She held out her hand for him to shake and he looked at it, and then at her, unable to move.

This could not be Lyla. The Lyla. His child bride. The scrap of a thing he had rescued six years ago.

She slowly lowered her hand after he failed to respond. Jules cleared his throat, and Brandi gasped loudly, probably shocked at his rudeness.

"Lyla Wiley," he murmured after a long drawn out pause where they both stared at each other. "You have grown up."

"Case Wiley," she replied in almost the same tone. "So have you. You look different. Better."

"You too." Case grinned and held out his hand.

Lyla took his hand in hers and smiled. "It's nice to meet you again."

A CASE OF LOVE

BRENDA BARRETT

A Case of Love

A Jamaica Treasures Book/February 2019
Published by Jamaica Treasures
Kingston, Jamaica

978-976-8247-69-8
Jamaica Treasures
P.O. Box 482
Kingston 19
Jamaica W.I.
www.fiwibooks.com

ALSO BY BRENDA BARRETT

FULL CIRCLE
NEW BEGINNINGS
THE PREACHER AND THE PROSTITUTE
AFTER THE END
THE EMPTY HAMMOCK
THE PULL OF FREEDOM
REBOUND SERIES
THREE RIVERS SERIES
NEW SONG SERIES
BANCROFT SERIES
MAGNOLIA SISTERS SERIES
SCARLETT SERIES
WILEY BROTHERS SERIES

ABOUT THE AUTHOR

Books have always been a big part of life for Jamaican born Brenda Barrett, she reports that she gets withdrawal symptoms if she does not consume at least two books per week. That is all she can manage these days, as her days are filled with writing, a natural progression from her love of reading. Currently, Brenda has several novels on the market, she writes predominantly in the historical fiction, Christian fiction, comedy and romance genres.

Apart from writing fictional books, Brenda writes for her blogs blackhair101.com; where she gives hair care tips and fiwibooks.com, where she shares about her writing life.

You can connect with Brenda online at:
Brenda-Barrett.com
Twitter.com/AuthorWriterBB
Facebook.com/AuthorBrendaBarrett

Chapter One

"Lyla Wiley! I have been calling you for the past fifteen minutes."

Lyla jumped. Brandi had unceremoniously pulled out her headphones and was talking loudly in her ear.

"But I should have known that you would be over here drooling over C. Wiley. You are so predictable. Girl, you have it bad."

Lyla dragged her eyes from her computer screen and focused on her roommate.

"What is it?"

Brandi grinned and waved two envelops in the air. "Nothing! Just the fact that we got in! We got in! We both got in!"

Lyla got up and squealed. "Yes!"

Brandi grabbed her, and they danced around the living room and then collapsed in hysterics in the overstuffed sofas.

"You are really related to the Wileys?" Brandi looked at

the dazed expression in her eyes. "I didn't believe you until now. I always thought you were just pulling my leg."

"I am a relative in a way, a distant way," Lyla said, pushing her hair from her eyes. "I was just as anxious as you to see if I would get in."

"Who would have thunk it?" Brandi got up and headed for her phone, her energy restored. "Brandi Phillips, management trainee. I have got to tell my mom. I can't believe that I am going to be working at Preston Wiley's office for the summer…the whole summer as a management trainee. Five months of training, whoop! Whoop!"

"My mother is not going to believe this." Brandi slapped her forehead and then handed her an envelope. "Sorry, here is your acceptance letter. Look at the pay. Look at it."

Lyla took the letter from Brandi and swallowed the lecture that was on the tip of her tongue about privacy.

It would not make a difference. It would sail straight over Brandi's head. It was a good thing that she rarely received regular mail.

She grabbed her computer and found that Wiley Supermarket had written her an email as well. She read the mail while Brandi gushed over the phone to her mother.

She tried to ignore Brandi's conversation, only tuning in when she heard her name.

"It has to be because Lyla has been pulling strings on the quiet Mom. You know Wiley Supermarkets was a long shot. They don't usually take third-year students in their management trainee program. I put Lyla as one of my references, and I got in."

Lyla watched Brandi enviously. She had a close relationship with her mother and a close-knit family.

Lyla had no one to call and no family. Contrary to Brandi's assumptions that she had some influence on the Wiley's, she had none. She stalked them on the internet, she pored over articles that mentioned them, and she watched any and every C. Wiley music video.

She had no more influence than a regular fangirl.

She knew nothing more about the Wileys than what they wanted the world to know. In the past she had badgered Sienna, her former guardian, about Case, but Sienna only knew what her son Jules told her and that was not much.

Lyla suddenly missed Sienna. She had been the only mother figure in her life. She was nurturing and caring, a true mother earth type who embraced everyone and loved all people but then cancer took her.

She hadn't been diagnosed long and then three months later she was gone.

Lyla sighed. She was alone. If she didn't get the regular deposits in her account every month and her school fees paid, no questions asked, she would even believe that Case had forgotten about her.

But as it was, she was well provided for. If she wanted anything extra, she would ask Rita Bloom, the lawyer in charge of Case Wiley's affairs. That is what Sienna had done when she was alive.

Lyla had to reluctantly make a call in her second year of university when Sienna had died, and she had nowhere to live.

Rita was efficient and brisk. She had been the one to help her set up her accounts. Rita had been the one who had found the two-bedroom furnished apartment that was a ten-minute drive from school and had supplied her with Brandi as a roommate.

Lyla had no idea how the apartment was paid for. She didn't pay rent or utilities. Case was her silent benefactor.

Obviously, no expense was to be speared where she was

concerned. She switched screens from her mail to look at his music video again.

She knew each of his features. She was obsessed with him and had been since she first saw him in Havana when she was fourteen years old.

He had been on stage, singing, My God is Awesome in Spanish, and she had felt every word.

She had fantasies of them meeting again now when she was an adult, of him falling in love with her and the two of them living as man and wife in the true sense.

Impossible dreams.

Case had saved her from a fate worse than death. Her mother would have sold her to Casa de Prostituta and to Havana's most notorious pimp if Case had not been moved enough to help her out.

She hit play on My God Is Awesome again and listened to Case's smooth rendition of the song.

"Can't you give the guy a rest for three minutes." Brandi chuckled. She had finished with her phone call.

"I know he looks good, but he is unattainable. Focus on the men in real life. Do you know how many guys on the university campus would give their left arm to go out with you? But you ignore them all."

Lyla grimaced. "I am not interested in the social scene until I have graduated."

"You are exasperating." Brandi sat beside her and glanced at the screen. "Take out the headphones. I want to hear him sing."

Lyla grinned. "You like him too."

"His voice is like honey, and his face." Brandi fanned herself. "Ooh child, when I see him in videos, I think, glory. No man looks this good in real life. He is probably short and has a bad temper."

"He is not short," Lyla said contemplatively. "He is tall, with skin like dark honey…the warmest kindest eyes, covered with eyelashes like fans, and the gentlest smile. He is gorgeous and humble at the same time."

"I want to see if this is really true." Brandi grinned. "We should go to his concert in Negril tomorrow."

"Negril?" Lyla raised an eyebrow.

"Yes, why not?" Brandi put on her determined face. "Adam has tickets. We can stay at his friend Jerry's house and then come back on Sunday, have a road trip weekend. We have just a week before we become working women."

"I hate going out with you and Adam. I hate being the third wheel."

"But you will do it because you want to see Mr. Handsome live." Brandi grinned cheekily. "Maybe we can even act as total groupies and go and see him backstage. Who knows? Maybe you can pretend that you two are related, you have that Wiley name, it seems to open doors."

****

Case was not having the best week. His manager Jules was in his ear about doing a Spanish Gospel album, and at the same time, he was booking him for gigs left, right and center. Case barely had time to breathe before he was off to some event or the other. Tonight he was in Negril after performing at two weddings, and he was feeling bone tired. His voice needed a rest.

He glared at Jules who was gleefully on the phone chatting to some promoter or the other about him.

"Yes, I know," Jules was saying in the phone. "He fills up a stadium better than any other single gospel artiste I have had the privilege to manage. Have you heard his song, God and Life? Everybody is jumping to cover it. Case wrote it himself. He is a very spiritual young man. The real deal."

Case closed his eyes tiredly and took deep soothing breaths. It was impossible not to hear Jules arranging yet another gig for him. It was also impossible for him not to hear the music coming from the stage at the venue. The artiste tents were relatively close to the stage. Somebody was performing a very lively medley of soca gospel songs. The artiste on stage sounded as if he had enough energy to spare for everybody.

Case didn't have much. He was running on fumes. He sang at two church services, and a wedding just today and he was the main act in an hour. The people came to the venue to see him. His song God and Life had taken over the airwaves. He had written it after Sienna Harvey's funeral. He had felt his mortality strongly at the time.

He had not been able to make it because he had been halfway across the world. He closed his eyes wearily, he felt like taking a nap, but he had sixty minutes of performing to do, and then he was heading back to Kingston.

He would sleep the day through and then take a mini vacation that week.

"What month is it?" He asked Jules tiredly.

Jules ended the phone call with a cheesy grin on his face. "April. Why?"

"My sister-in-law is going to give birth to twins this month," Case said, "and my lawyer says that my annulment is on track for the end of the month. April is going to be pretty busy."

Jules scratched his head. "You are really going through with the annulment without seeing your wife?"

"Yup." Case nodded. "Not interested."

Jules shook his head. "If you see Lyla now, you might change your mind about staying married to her."

"I won't," Case chuckled. "I am sure she is pretty. She was an attractive child. Even through that curtain of greasy curls and that emaciated body I could see her potential. If you are so interested in her why don't you pursue her after the annulment."

"I can't, Jules made a face. I love her, but not like that. She looks a lot like my mother, and my great grandmother. When I see her, I think family, not lover."

Case raised an eyebrow. "Lyla looks like Sienna?"

"Yep. It's in the eyes and the mouth." Jules grinned. "When people saw them together, they assumed Lyla was my mother's long-lost daughter or something. You may not have seen it because you never saw them together when she cleaned up, but the resemblance was wild."

Case nodded. "That must have been why she felt so familiar that night."

"Maybe," Jules said wistfully. "That resemblance is also why I still keep in touch. That and the fact that my mother made me promise to always look out for Lyla even when she would not be around. That's why I call her every two weeks or so. I always keep my promises. On our last phone call, she said she may swing by to hear you this evening. She is a fan."

"Really?" Case felt surprise and a strange curiosity that he tried to quash. Lyla was a fan. How did that make him feel? Why was he even feeling anything?

It was time he untied himself from Lyla. Not seeing her would make things much easier.

While he was pondering, Jules was talking. He only zoned in when he heard Barbados.

"So that's why when I promised the organizers in Barbados that you would show up at Gospel Fest this year, you have to do it. They are already promoting you, and this hit single that you just came out with is blowing up the airwaves. People want to see you live."

Case frowned. "I already said no to Gospel Fest. Wasn't it scheduled for tomorrow! What's wrong with you man?"

"It's a nine-day event," Jules said cajolingly. "You are booked for the last day. However, I told Collin, the organizer, that you will show up for the twenty-twenty celebrity cricket match. You like cricket, don't you?

"And that's just the first day. I also booked a luxury villa in Mullins Bay. It's called Sunset Villa, gorgeous place. You will have nine days of semi-vacation. I have you booked with three radio shows, two morning television shows and we are doing the music video for God is Life at the villa, Sunset villa is perfect for it. It has an excellent backdrop and an infinity pool, plus I have the production crew lined up over there. They do good work."

"And this is a vacation?" Case raised an eyebrow.

"Basically," Jules said, "there is never a dull moment in Barbados."

"I would say," Case muttered. "A luxurious vacation with my manager and personal assistant and a video crew."

"The video crew will only be there for a day," Jules smirked. "And then it will just be us, and the villa support staff. The villa has six bedrooms. If you want to carry a friend or three or five, it's doable. What's your nephew Pete doing these days?"

"He is in school. Pre-university." Case shrugged. "His parents would not pull him out of school for a week. He is doing very well in school."

"Good for him." Jules breathed. "But he is such a great singer too. He could make a go at this, be a touring singer like you, make lots of money, travel the world. I would manage him in a heartbeat."

"He is already making lots of money," Case snorted, "he designed a game app when he was sixteen, called Fruit Press."

"No," Jules widened his eyes. "Fruit Press is my downtime game. I spend lots of monies with in-app purchases. Your nephew has me hooked."

Case grinned. "It is addictive."

"Well then," Jules shrugged, "since Pete is out just know that if you want to invite a couple of people along for the ride, you can."

"Not going to happen," Case said. "For one, it's too short notice, and two Fifi is not here. She is the only person I want to spend down time with. We have never really done any of that. I spend more time with you than I do with her. I asked her to marry me before she went to Africa you know."

"I know, and I am still baffled by it. I don't know how you do it," Jules marveled aloud. "If I were planning to marry a woman, I would spend way more time with her in person than you do with Fifi. Phones and video sessions and all of that stuff cannot replace face to face and intimate contact. I don't get what you see in Fifi anyhow."

"I like her. She doesn't want or expect romance or any of that stuff. She knows what she wants out of life, and she goes for it." Case grinned. "I like her no-nonsense, no holds barred, no-frills approach to life."

"So do you feel passion and breathless anticipation when you are with her?" Jules asked curiously. "Have you two even kissed?"

"No, we are reserving the first kiss for when the minister says, you may kiss the bride." Case elevated his foot on a stool and sighed. "We'll be fine. I don't want to get caught up in passion or romance. I never want to lose my head over a woman. I love Fifi for that. She is just as level headed as I am. We will work."

Jules looked poleaxed, "I can't wrap my mind around it. I've been married twice, and both times, I remember the sense of the wonder the trippy heartbeat, the chemistry, the steamy nights, the sense of anticipation…"

"The divorces." Case finished Jules' sentence scornfully. "The drama, the quarrels, the double murders."

"Not murders. Not in my situation." Jules winced. "Why is it that out of all your brothers, you are the one that the murders affected the most? You were only a baby when it happened. All the others have moved on with good partners, and here you are speaking negatively about romance and all of the good feelings in life."

Case was saved from answering when the stage manager pushed his head through the door. "You need to get ready, Mr. Wiley."

Case threw a glare at Jules before he got up from the chair. "What Fifi and I have is none of your business, okay. I am fine. My life is fine. I am not the only man in the world that hates the very word romance. I am a proud pragmatist. I will never lose my head over a woman. Neither will I let lust or romance or whatever you call it cloud my judgment."

"Okay Mr. Pragmatist," Jules nodded. "I will stay out of your business, but please note that you are weird and whether you are a romantic or whatever, you need to spend time with your potential wife. That much I know."

"Fifi assured me she will be in Jamaica all summer; she wants to do a CD with me. So we'll be spending a lot of time in the studio."

Jules winced. "Can she sing?"

Case chuckled. "Not really, I'll get her a voice coach. We can make it happen."

Jules snorted and waited until Case walked out before

calling Saint Wiley.

"Hey Saint," Jules said after Saint answered. "I am calling as a man who has your brother's best interest at heart."

"I am listening," Saint said, his voice alert.

"Check out Fifi Daniels for me, please," Jules said grimly. "A thorough background check."

"What caused this sudden need to dig into Fifi's life?" Saint asked interestedly.

"I was in Miami last month and had a long talk with Sharla."

"Ah," Saint chuckled. "Sharla dislikes Fifi passionately."

"And she would know." Jules sighed. "She sees Fifi even more than Case. Your brother is always traveling. Fifi is always traveling.

"Fifi lives in Miami. His home base is in Jamaica. I was shocked when he said a couple of minutes ago that Fifi was coming to visit him in Jamaica, she never comes here to visit. He is always the one going to see her."

"Well, she has a large ministry based in Miami," Saint said after a pause. "And Case travels a great deal."

"They hardly see each other. I don't see why Case wants to marry her. He is young. He will fall in love one day. If he marries her, he will be tying himself up in a practical relationship without passion and spark. It could be his downfall."

Saint cleared his throat. "I don't want to interfere in how Case chooses his life partner. My brothers make their own mistakes."

"Usually I wouldn't interfere either," Jules murmured, "but I have a hunch. Call it a bad feeling in the pit of my stomach. Sharla confirmed that Fifi is not right for him and we need to know more about her."

"She is a pretty good preacher," Saint said, a smile in his

voice. "Have you ever watched her? My wife loves her down to earth approach to the gospel."

"No," Jules said sheepishly. "We've been so busy. Maybe I will take in a sermon this week when we are in Barbados and get some of the down to earth preaching."

"Barbados huh?" Saint said enviously.

"I would invite you and Sandrene," Jules chuckled, "but I hear that congratulations are in order. You are about to be a father."

"Thank you," Saint murmured. "Sandrene can't wait until they get here. She looks like she is about to pop and one of the girls is extremely active."

"You thought of names yet?" Jules asked. "Please think about it carefully. My mother named me Raphael from one of the archangels, and I never lived down the name."

"Your name is Raphael?" Saint laughed. "You are right; it doesn't suit you. I can't imagine you as an angel, Jules."

"Well, my mother was the one with the imagination. She named me Raphael Julius Harvey." Jules grumbled. "As early as age eight I told people my name was Raph. There was one girl who made it sound good though. She would call me Raphael with a thick Spanish accent and roll the r's and make it sound pretty, but she's the only one that I could stand calling me Raphael. So think about what you'll name your girls."

"Our girls will be called something with an S. We have a couple of possibilities lined up, but we are leaning toward Sienna and Sarah."

"My mother's name!" Jules smiled. "It would be lovely."

"Yes, I am glad you approve." Saint cleared his throat. "Now back to Case and his love life."

Jules chuckled. "His weird love life. Please send the check to me personally. I would not want Case finding out that I am doing this. He seems convinced that Fifi is the one for him and he needs no intervention because he is choosing her with his head and not his heart. And Lyla, gorgeous Lyla, his own wife, he hasn't even met her yet."

"This one is pro bono," Saint said abruptly, "and if I find anything Case is going to find out, whether he likes it or not."

Jules hung up the phone with a smile. That was the outcome he was hoping for; Case would take bad news about Fifi better from his brothers than from him. Assuming there was even bad news.

He was probably just overly suspicious of Fifi and her motives because he had always been protective of Case. He has been managing him from the lad was sixteen. In a way, he felt as if Case was closer to him than his family. He felt responsible for him in a way that he would a son, even though he was just thirteen years older than Case. He would probably be the closest thing to a son he would have anyway, especially after his brush with testicular cancer.

He got up and headed for the stage area. He liked to keep an eye on things in the wings where he could observe Case as he performed.

Chapter Two

Lyla was fuming when she entered the concert venue with Brandi and Adam. She almost missed Case's set. Adam had lent Jerry his car to go on an errand and Jerry had forgotten to take it back in good time.

She glared at Jerry who was standing beside her now. He was a tall, lanky fellow with a happy go lucky attitude and no regard for time. He took nothing seriously, and his mouth looked like he was always on the verge of a smile.

Lyla had only met him once before. He was Adam's second cousin. He lived in a neighborhood on the outskirts of Negril in his mother's four-bedroom house and worked as an entertainment coordinator at one of the hotels in the area. He was a shameless flirt. He called every female 'babes' and 'honey love'. His casual endearments annoyed Lyla.

"Babes, I apologize," he whispered to her for the thousandth time. "Please forgive me honey love."

"You are forgiven, Jerry," Brandi hissed. "We didn't miss

Case Wiley. If we had, Lyla would never forgive you."

Lyla nodded. "Brandi is right, and stop calling me honey love or babes or darling or whatever. My name is Lyla."

Jerry put a hand over his heart in a comical gesture. "My heart couldn't bear it if you hadn't forgiven me, honey… er…babes…honey…Lyla."

Lyla ignored him. Her attention zoned into the man on the stage. She wished that they could go closer, but they had arrived late, and it was a packed venue. She had to settle for viewing him on the two giant screens that were on the side of the stage.

"We are not going to get close to him tonight," Brandi whispered.

Lyla nodded. "It was a long shot anyway."

She tuned out Brandi, Jerry, and Adam and concentrated on Case who was performing hit after hit. He started with his livelier selections, and then went to the soul-stirring ones. He even went acapella with one of his songs, God and Life.

We never know what's in store with our life

Troubles, tribulations, accidents cause strife

Debt and death are certain, we just need to lift up the person,

The only one who made us, who took time to shape us…

One lady beside them was sobbing. "I love that song so much. And I love him!"

"He is still single," Brandi turned to the lady. "But you'll have to join a long, long, line."

"Brandi," Lyla hissed.

"What?" Brandi swung back to Lyla and giggled. "It's not as if you, or the lady or any of us will ever get a chance with him."

But he was not single. Not technically. Lyla thought longingly. Case Wiley was married to her.

She drunk in his features from the grainy screen. He had changed a bit. He looked more mature. Maybe it was the hairstyle, it was in a fade cut. The sides were low, the top higher in curly ringlets.

For one moment he looked directly at the camera, and it seemed as if he were staring at her. Lyla gasped.

But obviously, she was not the only one who thought so.

"Those eyes," Brandi murmured, "those soulful eyes. He is too cute for words."

"Ahem." Adam cleared his throat. "I am not about to get jealous at a gospel concert. Keep your lustful mind on the message of the song and not the singer, Brandi."

Brandi giggled. "I was saying it out loud for Lyla."

"He is not all that." Jerry cut in. "Look at me, Lyla. I have soulful eyes."

Jerry squinted and made a funny face.

Lyla smiled. "No talking. I like this song."

They were quiet for a while and then Case finished his set.

There was prolonged applause and people shouting encore.

Case returned for the encore and then the MC came on stage. They ended with prayer. The MC could barely utter amen before Brandi was dragging Lyla toward the stage area.

"Hey, you two are going in the wrong direction," Adam said. "Exit is that way." He hooked a finger toward the gate.

"We are going to say hello to Case," Brandi said. "Lyla knows him."

"I met him once at a concert in Cuba six years ago." Lyla groaned. "I doubt he will recognize me. I don't want to seem like a groupie."

"We are not groupies," Brandi insisted, "just one picture with him and then we are out of here."

"We'll wait by the car," Adam said. "I'll call you to remind you where we are parked."

"Cool." Brandi nodded and headed determinedly toward the stage.

Lyla followed Brandi's jeans-clad figure closely not wanting to lose her in the crush. She wished she had worn jeans like Brandi, but she had on a blue and ivory summer dress that fell just above her knee, and she had worn matching wedges. She had wanted to make a good impression on Case if they had gotten the opportunity to see him tonight. However, the uneven ground and the toe area of the wedge was causing some discomfort.

It was worth it if they saw Case tonight. She wanted him to see that she was no longer the scrawny kid that he had rescued from Cuba.

She had taken extra care with her wavy hair which was in healthy shape. It hit her a little below her waist. She had a spot on her right cheek from a left-over zit, but she had covered that with makeup, flawless makeup courtesy of Brandi who did bridal makeup in her spare time.

She had worn a brighter lipstick than she was used to, and she hoped that it was still intact and not on her teeth. She had bitten her lip more than once tonight.

She had also emphasized her eyes with heavier kohl than usual, but her eyes had teared up when Case had song the lines, I don't know what's in store for my life, but I am happy that God is in the strife.

Those were genuine words. She knew that he wrote his own songs. She had heard the emotions behind them, and she had teared up like a ninny.

She nervously wished that she had a mirror to make sure that she was okay. They entered the temporary dressing room area. Several security guards were fanned out around the space.

They had not had so many security personnel in when

Consuela had dragged her backstage in Cuba.

Lyla sighed. She knew this was a lost cause.

"Excuse me miss." One security said to Brandi. "This is a private area unless you have a backstage pass."

"Backstage pass?" Brandi widened her eyes, "you don't recognize me? I am CeCe Winans. I need to speak to C. Wiley. I have to find out why he is not using his first name. The abbreviations are only for my family."

The security laughed out loud. "That's a good one. You do look a bit like CeCe Winans. A very young CeCe Winans. How old are you?"

"Twenty," Brandi said.

"And your real name?" the security asked good-naturedly.

"Brandi Phillips and that's my friend Lyla Wiley." She pointed to Lyla who was trying not to look at them. She was not as bold as Brandi, and she never would be.

"Wow, very pretty lady," the security looked at her and smiled. "She's a Wiley huh?"

Lyla smiled back shyly.

"Yes, she is," Brandi said hopefully. "She is family. You can't turn away family."

"I still can't let you through," He said regretfully, "no matter how gorgeous you two ladies are. C. Wiley is a lucky man. I have had to turn away several women tonight who just had to see him or else they would die."

Lyla looked over at the restricted area and spotted Jules. He was talking to a man with a headset over his ears. She was about to turn away with Brandi when he spotted her.

"Lyla!" He waved vigorously. He walked up to the metal barriers and said something to the security guard and then he stepped aside.

"So you really are family, huh?" He said when she passed.

Brandi was beside herself with glee.

"Hey, you," Jules hugged her. "I didn't know you had decided to come. You could have traveled down with us."

He turned to Brandi, "and who is this?"

"This is Brandi, my housemate." Lyla grinned. "You've heard me talk about her."

"Yes, oh yes." Jules nodded. "My name is Julius Harvey. Everybody calls me Jules. Lyla and I go way back."

Brandi was staring at him with her mouth opened.

Lyla elbowed her before she snapped it shut.

"Nice to meet you." Brandi squeaked.

"Likewise." Jules inclined his head. "You want to see Case, don't you?"

"Yes please." Brandi breathed.

"Come with me," Jules grinned. "He will be surprised. How long has it been, Lyla?"

Six years, seven months," Lyla answered dutifully, knowing that he knew exactly how long it was.

He walked a little ahead of them toward the dressing room. It was close to the end of a long row of dressing rooms.

"Who is this Jules guy?" Brandi whispered. "He is cute. He has the cheekbones, the high forehead, the dark brown eyes. You know I like the clean-shaven bald head look with the neat goatee, especially on a dark-skinned man. Tall, dark and yum. Why didn't you tell me about him?"

"Jules is the son of my previous guardian. I never thought of him as cute. He is more like a brother to me." Lyla glanced at Brandi nervously. "You are going to behave yourself, aren't you?"

"Sure." Brandi nodded. "I am not thirsty. I have Adam, my boyfriend, since kindergarten and he is a looker. My man is fine too. When I get him to circle his beard and shave his head, he could give Jules a run for his money, minus the cheekbones and the height and the blindingly white teeth and the smooth voice. How old is Jules?"

Lyla chuckled. "Poor Adam. Jules is thirty-eight, or nine, I think."

"Give me a second, ladies." Jules turned to them and then walked into the dressing room.

"Is he single?" Brandi was practically licking her lips.

"I guess. Jules doesn't tell me anything about his relationships. When Sienna was alive, she used to lament about his ex-wives and how they had hurt him. I don't know what happened."

"Oh," Brandi said disappointment in her voice. "Older guy with ex-wife issues. Not one ex-wife but two. I'll pass."

"Good." Lyla grinned and then sobered up. "How do I look?"

"Gorgeous. Perfect." Brandi winked. "If I were the jealous type I would be jealous of you. As it is, I am confident in my own skin. Now go forth and wow the singer."

Jules came to the door, just when she said that. "Come on in, ladies."

Chapter Three

Case had his eyes closed. After the set he had come to the dressing room and sprawled out on the leather sofa. He was tired, and he needed a shower. After a set like the one he just performed he was usually wet and wrung out.

He was going to sleep all the way into Kingston tonight, but first he would go back to the hotel and shower. His black dress shirt was soaking; he unbuttoned it all the way down. He didn't have the energy to get up and shrug it off.

He heard Jules at the entrance of the dressing room talking to someone. He had no idea who, and he was past caring at this point.

He was visualizing the bed at his apartment. Shawn had recently decorated the place for him, and he liked it. He should spend more time there. His new bed was awesome and comfortable.

"Case," Jules' longsuffering voice invaded his thoughts. "Sorry ladies, it was a long day for him, and he sometimes acts like he is dead after a set."

Ladies? Case opened his eyes and looked over at Jules who was with company. Two girls were standing behind him.

The one closest to Jules was practically jumping in glee and clapping her hands in excitement. The other one was quite simply stunning. He had to blink several times before he could believe what his eyes were seeing.

He sat up in the chair, and both girls gasped.

"Yes, he works out." Jules grinned. "It helps him keep up his energy level while he's on stage."

Case made no move to pull his shirt closed. He cleared his throat. "Hello."

He was staring at her when he said it. How could he not? She was quite possibly the prettiest girl he had ever seen.

She smiled shyly. "Hi, Case."

"They wanted a picture and to meet their favorite singer." Jules was looking between him and the girl.

Case stood up. Suddenly he had renewed energy that he didn't known he had.

"Brandi and Lyla meet Case Wiley," Jules said.

"I am Brandi the excited girl waved to him. "Brandi Phillips. You are tall and even better looking in real life."

He smiled and shook her hand.

"And I am, er, Lyla Wiley." The other girl stepped toward him. She held out her hand for him to shake and he looked at it, and then at her, unable to move.

This could not be Lyla. The Lyla. His child bride. The scrap of a thing he had rescued six years ago.

She slowly lowered her hand after he failed to respond. Jules cleared his throat, and Brandi gasped loudly, probably shocked at his rudeness.

"Lyla Wiley," he murmured after a long drawn out pause where they both stared at each other. "You have grown up."

"Case Wiley," she replied in almost the same tone. "So have you. You look different. Better."

"You too." Case grinned and held out his hand.

Lyla took his hand in hers and smiled. "It's nice to meet you again."

Case nodded. He wouldn't release her hand. He held on to it for longer than was polite. He felt the softness of her palms, the slenderness of her arms. He wanted to pull her to him and attach her to him, limb for limb, sinew to sinew. He had never been so attracted to a woman in his life.

It was frightening.

And sudden.

And unexpected.

Like a blow.

He felt like rubbing his chest. His heart was beating rapidly. He also felt breathless, as if he had been running for a while.

He finally released her hand, and she rubbed it.

"Did I hurt you?"

"No, it's ah…" she swallowed visibly and then looked back at Jules and Brandi who was watching their byplay with rapt attention. "It's nothing."

Brandi cleared her throat. "We should go. Our dates are waiting for us outside."

Case stepped back reluctantly. She had come to his concert with a date. Jealousy bubbled inside of him thick and strong, which was shocking in and of itself. He never got jealous. He didn't even know he was capable of it.

"What are you doing this week, Lyla?" Jules jumped into the conversation swiftly. "I hardly see you anymore. Why don't you come to Barbados with us? All-expense paid. My treat."

Case widened his eyes and looked at Jules, but he did not protest.

"Can I come too?" Brandi whispered. "Like seriously, our exams just finished we have a week to go before we start working at Wiley Supermarket as business interns."

"Sure," Jules said. He turned to Lyla, "so what do you say? A week in Barbados. You can come with us tomorrow and leave Friday. That would give you the weekend to prepare for your new job."

"I ah," Lyla avoided looking at him, "I don't want to get in the way."

"You will not." Jules shook his head. "We just rented a six-bedroom villa, from all accounts it is huge and luxurious and trust me, you will not get in the way."

"Say yes." Brandi started jumping, "please!"

"I don't know..." Lyla looked across at Case. "Is this okay with you Case?"

"Sure." Case nodded. "Why wouldn't it be?"

He was pretending a nonchalance that he was far from feeling. He waited for her reply anxiously.

He wanted her to say yes, and yet he wanted her to say no. His emotions and thoughts were in an upheaval. He never expected, not in a million years, to be attracted to Lyla Martinez Wiley.

He hadn't expected to be attracted to anybody. Until now he had thought that he was immune from the regular male-female dynamics.

"Well then, yes." Lyla smiled at Jules. "We were not planning to leave Negril until tomorrow but…"

"Don't worry about it," Jules said. "We leave tomorrow afternoon. There is plenty of time for you and Brandi to go back to Kingston and pack. Remember to take your bathing suits. The villa has a pool, and there is a private beach behind the villa. I'll pick you up. I'll call you for the address."

Case pushed his hand into his pocket and rocked back on

his heels as she walked away. She gave him one last look before she left the dressing room. He didn't realize that he was holding his breath until she left.

"I told you she was gorgeous," Jules said and winked at him. "How did you like meeting your wife, Case Wiley?"

Case sat down on the settee he was occupying before Lyla walked into his life for the second time and upset his equilibrium. "I feel weird."

Jules laughed and then wiped his eyes. "I love it!"

****

"You and Case Wiley have enough heat between you two to sizzle," Brandi giggled when they were walking out towards where the vehicles are parked. "It's as if when you are both in the same room nothing else exists, no one else matters."

Lyla looked at Brandi. "You think so?"

Brandi nodded vigorously. "Oh yes, he remembered you from the first time you met too. You should have seen his expression when he saw you; he was stunned."

"And the feeling was mutual." Lyla smiled. Her hand was still tingling from where he had held it. She rubbed it absently.

"Good fortune follows wherever you go." Brandi clapped her hand. "I can't believe that I am going to Barbados. Like seriously, Barbados and I don't have to pay a dime."

Brandi jostled her with her elbow. "Hey, have I ever told you that it was a good day when I got to live with you. You know how it happened right?"

Lyla shook her head.

"I didn't have anywhere to stay when I got accepted to university. We were broke, couldn't afford anything else but part of the school fee, but my mother who is a prayer warrior got her prayer group to pray about it.

"Sis Verna is part of the group, and she said she felt impressed to call her sister Rita."

"My lawyer." Lyla smiled.

"Yup," Brandi nodded, "and lo and behold Rita said she was instructed by her client to find a place, it was a two bedroom, she didn't see any reason why I couldn't stay there rent free and bill free. My only stipulation was not to ask too many questions or be a bother to the client."

Lyla grimaced. "I didn't tell her to do that."

Brandi shrugged. "Maybe your sugar daddy did, isn't he the reason why you are not more excited about this Barbados trip. And isn't he the reason why you are so shy around Case Wiley. Everybody can see that you like him, and you are bowled over by him, but you are afraid to let it show."

"My sugar daddy?" Lyla widened her eyes.

"Yep." Brandi nodded. "I don't ask questions, and I never pry, but I jump to conclusions. And the conclusions I have drawn is that you are heavily monitored."

"Monitored," Lyla whispered.

"Yes." Brandi nodded. "Let's look at the facts. You never talk about your family except for Sienna who died. You mention Cuba once or twice, and then you clam up. And let's not overlook the fact that you have it made, you have your own car and apartment, you never worry about school fees. You never see any boys at school no matter the encouragement. You live like a nun."

Lyla stopped walking. "I don't have a sugar daddy."

"Oh yes you do," Brandi said with certainty. "I think he allows me to be at the house so that you are not alone, and I think," she lowered her voice, "that he is watching you. How else would you explain the fact that you just got the opportunity to go to Barbados, to be in the same space as

Case Wiley, your crush but you paused for a long time. You'll get in trouble with the sugar daddy, won't you?"

"No," Lyla whispered in horror.

"Don't worry, if he comes out of hiding and approaches me, my lips are sealed. Okay? I won't tell him or his goons a thing about you."

Lyla smiled. "You watch too much television."

"If it is not a sugar daddy," Brandi shrugged, "it's a super strict parent. Are you the child of a mafia don?"

"A mafia don?" Lyla asked incredulously.

"Yes, someone with Cuban ties. That's why you don't want to talk about Cuba. And you did say that was where you were born."

Lyla laughed. "Yes I was born in Cuba, but no, I have no mafia links."

"You even pronounce it, Kooba." Brandi said faintly, "just like a native."

"Spanish is my first language." Lyla reminded her. "I learned English six years ago!"

"I keep forgetting that." Brandi grimaced. "You sound better than our Econ teacher, Senor Garcia, and he has been living here for twenty years!"

"Senor Garcia came here when he was middle-aged," Lyla said patiently, "I went to school here, I learned to drop the accent because I wanted to be understood and I didn't want to stick out. I worked at it."

"How is it that you have the Wiley then?" Brandi asked curiosity heavy in her voice. "It's not exactly a Spanish surname."

"Not all Cubans have Spanish surnames," Lyla said patiently. "However, my full name is Lyla Martinez Wiley. I am a Wiley through marriage."

"Through marriage?" Brandi squealed in the night air.

"What do you mean through marriage? You are not married. You mean a stepdad?"

They reached the parking lot, and Lyla debated whether to tell Brandi. It's not that she had gotten orders never to tell anyone about being married to Case or that she couldn't trust Brandi. She didn't go around telling people about her past. Not even Sienna knew the extent of what she went through.

"Where have you two been?" Adam emerged from the shadows and asked impatiently.

"We went to see Case Wiley and guess what, we are going to Barbados!" Brandi recounted the meeting and the offer. Jerry and Adam looked at them with envy.

At least the discussion over her surname was forgotten for now.

Chapter Four

"**F**ifi this ministry is at war, and you can stop it. I am not going to tell you how to fight this battle, but you need to hear me out for a while." Esmerelda Gooden, associate pastor, and manager of the hospital ministries and general busy body marched into Fifi's office at ten.

She sat across from Fifi's desk. Her wig swinging as she pulled the chair even closer to the desk so that she could make her statements with emphasis.

It was a meeting that Fifi was not particularly looking forward to, Esmerelda was outspoken, and she was one of the old guards. One of the originals. One of the members who knew her when she was a young bride to Bishop Daniels.

She was also one of the few that was still on her side since Cory Daniels, Bishop Daniels' only son came back from the seminary and was making noises about taking over his father's legacy.

Fifi sighed. "Okay, Esme. Hit me. I have an eleven o'clock

meeting with the board so bear that in mind."

"I'll be brief." Esme crossed her legs daintily and looked at Fifi. "You are still young and attractive."

Fifi sighed. "Why, thank you, Esme."

"You have suitors, people who are interested in you." Esme leaned forward, her round face earnest. "You should get married. Pick someone, anyone. Yes, you expanded this ministry and did a better job than Bishop Daniels ever did. Yes, you can preach the word and expound on the word of God, but you are a woman, and Cory Daniels is recently married, and he has the last name."

Fifi restrained herself from rolling her eyes.

"You need to marry that Case Wiley. He proposed didn't he, before your Africa trip? All of us, except the prudes, think it's a good idea. Not even Cory can top that. The attention that young man would draw to this place if you tie the knot. Goodness, I think we would have to keep service every day of the week."

"The prudes?" Fifi raised an eyebrow.

"The people who think that your age difference is a huge factor." Esmerelda chuckled. "Child, you have been with an old man, I can't begrudge you the opportunity to be with a young one and that Case Wiley is a crowd puller. I can see this ministry's coffers overflowing with the green when this becomes his home base."

"I am not marrying Case because of the coffers or because I want to put one up on Cory." Fifi rested back in her chair. "I like Case. He is unlike any man young or otherwise that I have ever known. He is different."

"Uh huh." Esme nodded, "That's a good start. Marry him, bring him back here and let us all praise the lord."

Fifi chuckled. "Esme, Esme."

"Don't Esme me," Esmerelda looked at Fifi fondly. "I like

you. I know most of the people here have no idea what you went through in your younger years. How rough it was on you. I want to see you happy. Most of us were happy when the Bishop found love again. The first Mrs. Daniels had not been the best match, and when she died, we thought the Bishop would have been single forever."

Fifi sighed. "Okay, Esme. I appreciate this walk down memory lane but now is not the time."

"You should have had some kids for the Bishop or at least raised Cory because let me tell you, Fifi, he is out to get you. You have no idea how serious that boy is."

"I know he is serious and maybe he has a right to be." Fifi sighed. "But I do the most missionary work. Africa was a once in the lifetime experience. We touched so many lives, inspired so many persons…"

Esme cleared her throat impatiently. She had already heard about the wonders of the African continent.

"Have you looked in the mirror lately? You are a beautiful woman. You don't look your age either. That baby face look is working in your favor. You could easily pass for twenty-nine. I know I was fooled when the Bishop brought you to church and said you were his wife. I wondered where did the bishop get this child bride?"

"Esme…" Fifi groaned. "Please stop."

"No, no way," Esme shook her head. "You are supposed to be on a break, you need a vacation. Go to Jamaica or wherever Case Wiley is now and get moving with this relationship. I don't see this moving anywhere if you keep jetting off to Africa and God knows where. Don't let this be a twenty-year engagement. I doubt if you have twenty days. Cory has been talking to the board members. He is going to move for a motion of no confidence against you. He argues that you are single and a woman. That little runt is even using the Bible to justify the women can't be church leaders' stance. You have to stop him."

Esme looked at the calendar on the desk and frowned. "You are going to Barbados for the Women in Gospel talk later this week. And Cuba? You were planning to go to Cuba after?"

"Yes." Fifi felt jittery, Esme was right, she was sliding on thin ice with Cory breathing down her neck. "Quick family trip, I have not been back in years. I think it is time I went back and faced some demons. This trip is not a business one; this is strictly personal."

Esme frowned. "Why don't you do that after your wedding? Have a honeymoon there? Cuba is beautiful. I remember when Stan and I went to Havana. It was gorgeous, and we spent a couple of days in Varadero. Oh my goodness, it was lovely. And then there was Trinidad. I had no idea there was a place in Cuba called Trinidad. Quite near there was this place called La Boca. Have you heard of it?"

"Yes." Fifi gritted out. "Esme listen…"

"Such a beautiful island, Cuba." Esme shook her head. "I would go back now at the drop of a hat. Stan would too. We had fun."

Fifi shook her head. When she went back, it had to be alone. She wanted no one around when she visited the past.

Esme frowned. "You never talk about your life in Cuba, and we have so many Latinos here, that is such a shame. I had a neighbor once, he couldn't shut up about it. His adventures in his village, the food, the fun…He lived on a coffee farm in the hills; his family were one of the few that actually owned the land because most of it is government owned and he had the…"

"Esme give me a break!" Fifi said in exasperation, cutting off her friend in mid-sentence. She knew Esme was fishing for details about her life in Cuba.

One time a long time ago now, she had mentioned that she had a rough couple of years with her family, after that Esme's imagination had run wild.

"Okay, okay, I know I am obvious, but Cory has been saying some things about you and your time in Cuba." Esme sniffed. "He says if it comes out, you'll embarrass us all."

"He said that?" Fifi gasped. "He is such a…How can he claim a moral high ground? He paid two girls to have abortions while he was in the seminary and he can't keep it in his pants. The hypocritical busy body will cause more scandals if he is in charge than anything that he can dig up about my past."

Esme winced. "He said he was just a man and that he confessed his sins and the Lord has forgiven him."

"And yet, my supposed sins are not forgiven?" Fifi sneered. "Because I am a woman? Give me a break. I don't want to speak ill of the dead, but I made most of the decisions for the Bishop while he was alive. It was all me. I've been running this place long before the Bishop passed. At times he had no idea which way was up or down, his mind was gone."

"I know that," Esme said. "Trust me, most of us on the board do, but thirty-eight of the fifty board members are men. They want to see you married and frankly so do I. Promise me you will spend some time with Case Wiley. Take him to Cuba with you if needs be."

"I was planning to spend a couple of weeks in Jamaica this summer." Fifi shrugged. "I want to do an album, Shirley Caesar style."

"Well this summer is too late, Esme rummaged in her bag for her cell phone. "Invite him to Cuba with you."

"No," Fifi growled. "Esme you are beyond irritating now."

"The Holy Spirit is impressing me that you should make a

move now," Esme said smugly.

"The Holy Spirit?" Fifi widened her eyes, "I don't believe this!"

"Yes. The Holy Spirit." Esme scrolled through her phone, "If you don't move you are going to be relegated to an associate pastor, preaching only occasionally and probably overseeing the African ministry that you started. Cory would like nothing better than to have you in his shadow."

"I have a number for Case, but it's his booking number. Do you have a personal one?"

"Yes, but I am not giving it to you," Fifi said smugly. "I guess your meddling stops now, doesn't it?"

Esme pressed the number on her phone and looked at Fifi, a determined thrust to her chin. "We'll see. God works in mysterious ways."

"Oh hello," she said when a male voice answered. "This is Esmeralda Gooden from the Hope Ministries. Is there any way I can speak to Case Wiley directly? I am sitting in Fifi Daniels' office and I want to arrange a meeting with both of them."

Fifi struggled to decipher what was said on the other line. Esme was nodding and saying, hmmm. She even grabbed a pen and a paper and started jotting down information.

"That's interesting," Esme puckered her brow. "Fifi has a slot for the weekend too."

She listened some more and then declared. "That's perfect."

She hung up the phone and looked at Fifi smugly. "Barbados. That's where Case will be for the week. You would have known that if you two were closer. I just spoke to somebody named Jules Harvey. His manager, I presume. He said that there is space at the villa where Case is staying if you want it."

"Oh, Esme." Fifi sighed.

"Stay with Case in Barbados." Esme urged. "I know it in my bones that this is the best thing to do. Do a quickie wedding on the beach. I won't be mad at you if you don't invite me."

"I don't know about that, Esme."

"Do it." Esme pointed at her warningly. "Cory is winning!"

Marriage, Fifi drummed her fingers on the table. She needed to spend some quality time with Case before that happened or did she?

There were some things she needed to be honest with him about. That could come with time. She should have confessed when he had casually proposed, and she had just as flippantly said yes.

They needed to see more of each other to be in each other's space. In that regard, they didn't know each other that well.

Case wasn't particularly expressive emotionally, and he liked that she wasn't either. Theirs would not be a passionate love match if they ever tied the knot. They didn't have fire or chemistry, but they understood each other and were friends. That was what she thought he wanted.

In that way, they were super compatible.

But now she wasn't sure that she wanted a friendly marriage. She had already gotten that from the Bishop. She wanted something different. She wanted what she had for a brief moment a long time ago in Cuba.

It was the foolishness of youth. It couldn't be repeated. Those moments had to happen without the benefit of age and wisdom.

"I'll call his manager myself then." Fifi grimaced. "I might stay overnight. I am sure Case will be busy."

"But at least you two will be in the same space," Esme said smugly.

****

The incessant ringing of the doorbell was what dragged Case from a deep sleep on Sunday morning. He sleepwalked to the door, glancing at the clock on the way and then dragged his door opened. He was not surprised to see Saint standing there with an unrepentant smirk on his face.

"It is eleven o'clock," Saint said, "why are you still sleeping?"

"Late night," Case croaked. He headed to his sofa and laid on it, closing his eyes. "Thanks for waking me up though, I should be getting ready for Barbados. What's up?"

"Nothing much." Saint sat across from him. "I just thought I should tell you that Preston asked me to investigate Lyla Wiley. He saw a job application from her and he asked me to look into her past et cetera."

"Uh huh," Case said dreamily. "Lyla, she came up in a dream or two last night. She has grown up into an amazing looking woman."

"I thought you didn't know her," Saint murmured. "And you didn't want to because you were so in love with Fifi."

"I am not in love with Fifi. I think she and I would be perfect together." Case mumbled. "She is a powerful evangelist; I am a gospel singer. What could be better?"

"I don't know," Saint snorted, "love, caring, compatibility? You can't choose a life partner because she can preach. Neither should she choose you because you can sing."

"There is more to it than that," Case murmured, he was drifting away on a little white cloud.

"I am going to investigate her," Saint's voice seemed like it was coming from afar. "Like I investigated Lyla. I have my hands full at the moment but expect a full report in a few months.”

Case was falling back to la la land. He was almost in that sweet spot where he had not a care in the world when he heard Saint ask, “How much do you know about Lyla?”

“Not much,” he didn’t know if he said it out loud.

“She was born in Havana Cuba to Valentina Martinez. Valentina left her to be raised by her mother when she was a baby. Lyla grew up with her grandmother, Consuela Martinez.”

“Yes, I recognize that name,” Case murmured. “Consuela. I thought she was the mother.”

“No, she was not. Consuela was a well-known prostitute in Havana. She was the one who sold Lyla to you.”

Case cracked one eye open and tried to focus on Saint. “You don’t say.”

“Our guy in Cuba says Consuela has steady men friends that she entertains through the year. Apparently, it is the family business. Her daughter Valentina was an exotic dancer in a nightclub.”

“A dancer is not a prostitute,” Case murmured. “And Lyla was not a prostitute. You said family business as if she was a prostitute. When since you started jumping to conclusions detective?”

“Lyla missed it because of you.” Saint steepled his fingers under his chin. “But Valentina must have supplemented her income with customers, that’s what the women did at that particular club.”

“Stop jumping to conclusions. Lyla missed that lifestyle because of God.” Case got up and ran his fingers through his hair. “I felt an urge to get her out of there. Marriage was the quickest way to do it.”

“You said you met her recently?” Saint raised an eyebrow.

“Yes, last night.” Case got up. “I need some water; my

throat is dry. Want some?"

"No thanks." Saint watched him as he gulped down three glasses of water and then raised an eyebrow. "And?"

"And what?" Case grinned.

"And how was it? Meeting her for the first time since you rescued her?"

"I was in shock. Still am, to be honest. She's really pretty. Jules invited her to Barbados for the week. She'll be coming with us."

Saint smiled. "I see."

"Don't look so pleased. It's not as if I am going to start something with her."

Saint chuckled. "Okay. I believe you. You are anti-romance and anti-feelings. I know you are not going to fall in love with your wife."

"That's right." Case said, his voice sounding uncertain.

Chapter Five

Sunset Villa

Lyla looked out at the sea and the landscape from the front of the villa and then at Brandi, a cheesy grin on her face. They really were in Barbados with Case Wiley. Lyla had not shaken the sensation that she was dreaming from Saturday night. She had a red mark on her arm where she had pinched herself for the last couple of hours.

They had a driver meet them at the Grantley Adams International Airport, and she had been equal parts fascinated with the scenery and equal parts fascinated with Case. He had slept through the whole journey. It was obvious he was operating on autopilot. Jules, on the other hand, had been bright and chirpy and had kept them entertained.

Case sleepily smiled at her before they entered the villa. She smiled back at him. He looked adorable when he was half sleepy. His hair was ruffled and his eyelashes droopy. His eyes which already had a sleepy slant to it looked even more so.

She had learned a few things about him today. He could sleep standing up. She had seen it with her own eyes. He didn't snore, and he could hold a half sleepy conversation. Something that Jules took advantage of. He had Case agreeing to all sorts of things while he was out.

The enthusiastic housekeeper greeted them and offered to show them around. She introduced herself as Shannon. There was a bellhop/gardener/security personnel named Neil who stood behind her silently waiting for orders.

"Just show me where to crash," Case said his voice still sleep heavy.

"Of course, Sir," the housekeeper grinned. "I must say that I am a fan. Welcome to Barbados. Mr. Cameron said that you should have the suite to the right. You have a beach view, a private balcony, and a curved walk-in shower with a private spa and garden."

"Uh," Case nodded. "Where is the bed?"

Brandi giggled beside her. "I feel like that too."

"Your rooms are also upstairs." The housekeeper smiled. "There is one-bedroom downstairs, Mr. Harvey requested it."

"Jules! The name is Jules, Shannon. Not Mr. Harvey." Jules paid the driver and then turned to them. "Okay, show Case the way so that he can sleep."

"Dinner is at seven; it will be served on the back balcony," Shannon said when Case preceded her up the stairs.

She hurried after him.

Lyla and Brandi looked at each other and followed.

Lyla's room was spacious and cool. The whole place was cool. She belatedly worked out that there was central air conditioner when she opened the balcony door and the heat came in.

Brandi was in the room next to hers and shared a balcony. She was investigating at the same time as Lyla, they both opened their doors at the same time.

"I love this. Brandi inhaled. "I should go for a swim. The water looks inviting."

Lyla nodded. "Okay, meet you downstairs in three minutes."

On her way down she met Jules, who was as usual on his phone pacing up and down the spacious downstairs area as if he had urgent business.

He hung up when she came near him and shook his head. "You look so much like my mom. Even in the way you walk."

Lyla chuckled. "People told us that all the time. Sienna would say that we are all related because we are humans and have one creator."

Jules chuckled and then sighed. "I miss her."

"Me too." Lyla nodded.

"I wish I spent more time with her when she was in the land of the living." Jules grimaced. "Maybe I would have if I had stuck to medicine."

"You were in medicine?" Lyla widened her eyes. "You?"

Jules laughed. "Yes. Me. I did a year at the Latin American School of Medicine in Cuba. My mother was so proud of me. I won a scholarship and went to Cuba and then one night I went to Old Havana and heard the group Los Cantantes in a disco hall. There were about twenty of us in the place, and they were so good. They performed like their audience was twenty thousand. I mean pure salsa music."

"I know Los Cantantes." Lyla widened her eyes. "My mother played their album La Música es Mi Vida every day."

"Yes, they were good. Good enough so that I gave up my scholarship and any hopes of a medical career. I thought the world needed to hear them and I was going to be the one to help make it happen. Jules laughed. I still manage them. They don't tour as much now, but they are really popular in the Latin American world."

"That's why Sienna said you were compulsive." Lyla raised a brow at him. "She lamented that her only son was not into settling down, it bothered her."

"I settled down plenty," Jules grinned, "I married twice. Both times I 'settled' down. Both times it was not the best decision I had ever made. But then again, I was a little wild in my youth. I was totally unlike Case who was more responsible at nineteen than I had ever been. If I told you some of the things I got up to when I lived in Cuba…"

Brandi chose that moment to come down the stairs. "You lived in Cuba, Jules?"

"For a year." Jules chuckled. "I will tell you my grand adventures at another time. Maybe at dinner tonight."

"Looking forward to it." Brandi sniffed. "Lyla never talks about Cuba."

Jules grimaced. "Maybe she has reason not to."

Jules excused himself as his phone rang again.

Lyla and Brandi headed to the back patio and the beach beyond the walls.

"Oh, you are so full of secrets." Brandi hissed when they were on the powdery white sand. "Secrets, secrets, secrets."

"I don't deliberately have secrets." Lyla took off her lacy crochet bathing suit cover-up and sat on her towel. "I just don't talk about my past."

Brandi did the same and grunted. "I talk about mine all the time. I am not proud of everything that I have done but I see no reason to hide stuff. I don't know what the mystery is about. You said Saturday night that you are a Wiley by marriage. Whose marriage? Your mother's?"

Lyla chuckled. "My mother Consuela Martinez was

married to no one. She was a girlfriend."

"A girlfriend?" Brandi knitted her brow. "What's that?"

"Not quite a prostitute, just a girlfriend to whichever man came to our country and wanted a steady relationship for the time he was there. She had five or six of them, and she rotated them for the year. That was her profession. She never peddled in the streets; she had boyfriends. She took them to our one-bedroom apartment. Sometimes she went to whichever hotel they were staying. "She loved going to the hotels. When she left, I was usually on my own with nothing to eat. I was at the mercy of my neighbors the Alvarez's."

"Ooh." Brandi opened her mouth. "Ooh, I see."

"I hardly saw her." Lyla looked at Brandi's shocked expression and chuckled. "And then one day, her boyfriend from Canada took a liking to me, he was staying over the house, and he said I was more to his taste than her. I don't know who she was angrier at, me or the man. I never did anything to encourage him. I was just fourteen years old and despite having a mother like her still incredibly sheltered. My neighbors were Christians you see. Mrs. Alvarez was a music teacher, and Mr. Alvarez was a doctor. They had daughters my age and Mrs. Alvarez knew what my mother did. She always tried to intervene."

Brandi swallowed. "So what happened after the Canadian man?"

"Consuela told me to get dressed. When I did, she frog-marched me down the street with her hand on my ear twisting it and screaming, Puta! Puta! I'll show you what it means to be a puta!"

"And puta means?" Brandi was looking at her wide-eyed.

"Whore." Lyla shrugged. "I can remember the hunger. We hadn't eaten yet. My mother had lost it before dinner. She was screaming at me and then she said the words, prostituta, and Santiago. Locally we all knew that Santiago kept women, for male tourists who wanted them young."

Brandi shuddered. "Goodness."

"It was an open secret in Havana." Lyla shrugged. "I started praying. Senor Alvarez taught us how to pray. He said that God answered the biggest requests if we had just the tiniest faith. And I thought of the biggest thing that I could ask. I asked God to get me out of Cuba. I loved my country but hated my situation and wouldn't you know it, on the way to Santiago's place, they had a concert."

"A concert?" Brandi raised a brow, "I thought that you had to hide to attend those things in Cuba."

"In previous years you couldn't. A lot has changed since." Lyla shrugged. "They were at the Museum of the Revolution. It was packed. Case was singing My God is An Awesome God, and my mother dragged me over there and actually stood and listened, and then when he was done, she dragged me around to the dressing room where he was and offered me for sale."

"Say what?" Brandi gasped.

"Jules was there." Lyla chuckled. "He was the one who suggested that Case get married to me and get me out of the country. It was an answer to prayers."

"But, woah…" Brandi shook her head.

"Yep." Lyla nodded, "my mother agreed. She was happy to get rid of me. The papers were drawn up the next day. We went to city hall, and I was married."

"To Case Wiley?" Brandi rounded her eyes.

"Yes." Lyla nodded. "The day after that I came back to Jamaica with him and Jules and then I stayed with Sienna."

"But…" Brandi shook her head. "You are Case Wiley's wife?"

Lyla nodded.

"I can't believe this," Brandi muttered. "I have fallen asleep. I am still upstairs. I am having one of those lucid dreams where everything seems real, but it's actually not. Any minute now I am going to wake up. No, maybe I am not upstairs, maybe I am still at the townhouse in Kingston, and it's Saturday night."

Brandi snapped her fingers wildly. "Wait, so if I am here then Saturday night did happen. That's why the meeting between you and Case looked so strange. He was seeing you for the first time since Cuba?"

"Yup." Lyla nodded.

"How romantic," Brandi clapped her hands gleefully. "He was in awe. He did a double take. He was smitten. Like a knock to his head. He only had eyes for you, as far as he was concerned Jules and I were not in the room."

"Case does not like me like that," Lyla said depreciatingly. "I highly doubt he is having any feelings toward me romantic or otherwise."

"You didn't see what I saw Saturday night. That is if Saturday night did happen and I am not having a long lucid dream, right now."

Lyla got up. "Let's go swimming, that should wake you up."

"I hear you, Mrs. Wiley." Brandi grinned.

Chapter Six

Case woke up from what was a refreshing nap, and now he felt rested. He had a quick shower and followed the scent of vanilla and spices to the open plan kitchen area. Jules, Brandi, and Lyla were already sitting at the table. Shannon was at the stove. She was the first one to spot him.

"Mr. Wiley! I am happy you are up. Mr. Jules said you needed your rest, but I hated to serve flying fish and cou cou cold. It's not the same."

Case smiled. "Well consider me up and hungry. Ravenous actually."

His eyes met Lyla's, and he struggled to drag them away from her. It was proving to be impossible. How could she have gotten prettier?

She was in a filmy red top; her hair was parted to the side in large curls. She had mascara around her eyes, which made them appear bigger and more luminous.

She smiled at him, holding his stare.

Jules cleared his throat. He was looking between the two of them. Brandi snickered, and even that didn't break the spell.

It was Shannon who came between them with a serving dish in hand. "Mr. Wiley, I hope you enjoy our national dish. I make all my dishes with love."

He dragged his eyes from Lyla's and sat down across from her. "I am sure I will enjoy it, Shannon."

Shannon served them and then smiled. "I'll be back to serve dessert, which is black cake. I also have some mauby drinks if anybody wants to try out a real Bajan drink."

"I will." Jules nodded. "I acquired a taste for mauby years ago."

"You have been everywhere." Brandi chuckled. "Like everywhere!"

"That's right." Jules nodded, "the Caribbean is my backyard. Case's too."

"Yep." Case nodded. He tucked into his food. The flying fish was spicy, and the cou cou was creamy.

Case closed his eyes after the first bite. "I think this is the best fish I have ever eaten. Anywhere."

Jules laughed. "Nobody can go wrong serving you fish."

He turned to Lyla. "Can you cook it? Because that is the way to Case's heart. Fried, steamed, baked, roasted brown stew…"

Lyla started blushing. She looked at Case shyly and then over at Jules. "Of course I can cook fish, my mom taught me."

"Which one?" Case asked curiously. "Your grandmother Consuela or your mother?"

Lyla sat up straighter in the chair and looked at him with confusion. "I don't understand. I have one mother— Consuela Martinez."

"So, she never mentioned Valentina Martinez, her daughter

to you?"

"Yes," Lyla nodded, "but Valentina is my sister. She left for the US when I was a baby. She was a very good daughter to Consuela she would consistently send money to her every month. That is how we survived. She stopped for a while and then Consuela had the brilliant idea to sell me after her lover made a pass at me."

Jules glanced at Brandi and raised an eyebrow.

"I know all of this." Brandi shrugged. "I know she is married to Case and that she was sold and all of that high drama. I guess I am finally in the loop now. You don't need to whisper around me."

Jules sighed. "Well okay then. Did Lyla tell you I had testicular cancer and that is why my second wife divorced me?"

"No." Brandi shook her head. "Are you cancer free now?"

"Yes," Jules nodded, "but sterile."

"Jules," Case said in exasperation, "we are talking about Lyla. He turned to Lyla. I wonder why Consuela lied to you."

"I wonder why she did anything." Lyla sighed. "That she is not my mother explains a lot."

Jules cleared his throat. "You okay?"

"I am good," Lyla shrugged. "I kind of put all of the stuff that happened to me in Cuba behind me, you know. Consuela was not the best parent. She was violent; sometimes, her favorite weapon of choice was her high heels. At other times she carried her boyfriends to the house, and I had to sleep elsewhere. I had to find my way. I have been on my own since I was six."

Case winced. "That young, huh."

"Yup, I grew up rough." Lyla nodded. "How did you know about Consuela?"

"My brother owns a security firm. He investigated you

when I told them that I got married to you in Cuba. Case smirked. My brothers are overprotective. If you want, I can have him track down who your parents are."

"I don't care," Lyla said a forlorn quality to her voice. "I don't intend going back to Cuba ever. I guess that is where my father would be, and as for Valentina, if she is my mother and anything like Consuela, I think I am better off out of their lives."

"I had loving parents." Case looked at his fork and then back at Lyla. "When I was six, my father's wife, shot my mother and my father and my aunt and then shot herself. I heard it happening."

"Goodness." Brandi breathed.

Lyla widened her eyes. "Wow."

"She left behind nine orphaned children. Six for my dad and three for my aunt. My aunt's husband had already died. My brothers became my parents," Case said, "especially the oldest two, Preston and Jordan. They were all I had. No mother, no father. Just us."

"And you came out okay," Jules said jovially to lighten the mood.

Brandi and Lyla were staring at him with varying degrees of shock.

Case shrugged. "It is what it is, but sometimes in the middle of the night I wake up with a yearning to know them. I don't remember them properly. I see pictures, I hear stories, but I never had the opportunity to get to know them, like Jordan and Guy. They are the brothers I share both mother and father with."

Then Case realized how maudlin he sounded and switched the topic easily. "Jules, tell us about your adventures in the Caribbean and lighten up the mood here."

Lyla opened her mouth to protest. She was staring at him

with much compassion in her eyes which was unfair because she probably had a worst time than he had growing up.

His original circumstances were ugly, but his brothers had made sure that his growing up was more than bearable. They had never once gone hungry. He didn't know what deprivation was. No one had ever sold him to a stranger for a hundred US dollars.

"Do you want me to start from Anguilla, move on to Barbados, and then tackle Cuba?" Jules intruded on his thoughts. Case lost eye contact with Lyla who was chewing her food contemplatively.

"Tell me about Cuba," Brandi said, "I want to visit. Lyla never talks about it."

Jules chuckled. "I spent a year there for school, and half of it was about booze and women. I knew all the party places, and I did some wild stuff."

"That is not fit for polite company," Case said wryly. "And it's all a part of your past since you are now converted. Remember?"

"Yes." Jules nodded. "You are right. Thanks for reminding me, Case. My former life is now but a haze of smoke like the fat cigars I used to happily puff on back in the day, except for Maria, my first love. She and our one night together, I'll never forget."

Brandi giggled. "What was so memorable about that night?"

"Love at first sight," Jules said fondly. "It is exactly as the romance books say. Sharp and pointed. It felt as if we lived a lifetime that night. And that's all I'll say about that."

"Thank God." Case murmured.

Brandi chuckled. "So how did you end up being Case's manager?"

"It was after wife number two. My mother's church had a

variety show. I was recently baptized and looking around for Christian acts to represent."

"He was there. He was just a kid maybe around fifteen, and he had the audience eating out of his hands. My mother said to me that she dreamed about him before she saw him and that he would change my life. So I went to his brother Preston and asked him to give me a year to make him professional, and the rest they say is history. He did change my life."

They chatted some more. Case realized that Lyla eagerly lapped up all the little nuggets about him that Jules was so freely handing out. She stared at him so much he had caught her on more than one occasion, which meant that he was often looking in her direction.

Shannon came back to clear the table and offered them black cake. Which was heavy with rum and fruit. They could smell it from the moment she took it out of the cupboard.

Brandi declined a serving.

"I am so sleepy; I don't know if I can make it up the stairs." She left them to it.

Jules excused himself and took a call.

"My ex." He grimaced and took the cake with him. "This could get long and messy. I stopped paying spousal support when she remarried. Now she is in a hissy fit. The new husband is strapped for cash."

Case and Lyla were left alone.

"I don't want to get drunk," Lyla said sniffing the cake and tentatively taking a bite.

Case laughed. "I doubt that, unless you are very lightweight. Want us to take this to the poolside?"

"Sure." She smiled and got up.

He could hear the sea lapping on the shore from where they were. He could barely make it out in the dim light. He inhaled. It was a balmy night, the kind of night that would usually have him introspective and thinking up lyrics to songs. However, the only thing that came to his head was Lyla. Lyla in the red dress who smelled like cotton candy who loved to give him warm smiles. He was tempted to write a love song.

"What does Lyla mean?" He asked when they settled in two loungers at the poolside.

"Island girl," Lyla answered promptly. "I looked it up."

"Mine means container," Case grimaced. "It was supposed to be Casen, my brother Jordan said that my mom liked Casen, but my dad wasn't feeling it. So they took a family vote, and the final result was Case."

Lyla chuckled. "I like both of them, Case and Casen."

"I live with it, don't particularly like either of them." Case grimaced. "I use C. Wiley for work. Don't like my middle name either."

"Dominic." Lyla chuckled. "I think you and Jules are too picky about your names. They are good sounding names."

"And how do you know my middle name is Dominic?" Case turned to her.

"The marriage certificate." Lyla grinned. "I have a copy."

"Yes." Case chuckled. "I almost forgot about that. One hot night in Cuba six years and seven months ago I got married to Lyla Martinez."

"Do you encounter situations like mine all the time?"

"No." Case chuckled. "Never before you and never after. That was a dramatic one off. I usually go to a venue to perform and then go back home."

"Do you love it? The music? The touring? The adoring crowds?" Lyla asked. She was looking at him in the half dark interestedly.

The air between them was sizzling. Case could feel it, and he marveled at it. He had never had this reaction to a woman.

She was his wife. The thought crept into his head, and it wouldn't leave. What if he got to know her better? Maybe they could stay married? And what about Fifi?

He couldn't forget Fifi.

Fifi was the woman he had chosen with his head. She didn't inspire any feelings of passion within him. And he was almost sure he didn't inspire any in her either. And that was fine. Above all else, he didn't want to have any drama in his life. He got enough passion and purpose from music.

Music would be his mistress.

"Case?" Lyla jolted him back to the conversation.

"I love music. I have been doing it for as far back as I remember. Touring pays the bills, it gets tiring sometimes, but I rarely complain." He grimaced. "Of course, Jules would say I complain a lot. As for the adoring crowds, it doesn't affect me that much. My brothers have a way to bring me back to earth if I ever let it get to my head."

"Tell me about them." Lyla turned fully to look at him; she licked her lips, and he followed the movement dazedly.

"My brothers, uh…they are cool. Preston is the head of the Wiley Group and the supermarket. He is a humble person. I hang around with him the most out of all my brothers, which is ironic because he is more of a father figure in my life and he worries about me, and it can get annoying."

"Your story is fascinating," Lyla whispered. "I read snippets of it in a magazine one time, and I could barely believe it. You and your brothers are amazing."

Case chuckled. "We are just ordinary boys who found ourselves in extraordinary circumstances. And we made it work. Well, they made it work. I was the recipient because I was the baby."

"And now all of them have their own families?" Lyla said wistfully.

"Yup all paired up and domesticated." Case grimaced. "I don't believe in romance and that sort of stuff. I don't think I'll ever do what they did. To be honest, I think it is a little risky to join yourself to somebody just because of love. I think compatibility and maturity are more important."

Lyla looked at him sharply. "I see."

Case laughed. "You sounded like a prudish school mistress when you said, 'I see'."

"No, I didn't." Lyla chuckled. "I agree with you to a point, but I want love and romance and all the other ridiculous things that come with courtship. I want it all."

"I see." Case mimicked her voice, and she laughed.

"Have you ever dated anyone at school?" Case asked curiously.

"Yes, I almost had a boyfriend." Lyla shook her head. "I was a first-year student; he was graduating. It didn't work out. Besides, I didn't want to complicate things, you know. I am technically married."

"I know." Case leaned back in his chair. "I never intended for that to be a chain around you. I was kind of hoping that you'd forget about it and live your life."

"I couldn't. Maybe if I were married to somebody else but I…" she bit her lip. "What about you? Have you dated anyone?"

"I have a fiancée," Case murmured. "Asked her to marry me last year. The problem is, I haven't seen her in person since I asked her."

Lyla gasped. "Oh, I had no idea. How is it that you haven't seen her?"

"She was in Africa." Case ran his fingers through his hair. "Listen, I think we should get an annulment and then move on. I need to set you free. I don't want to hamper you with this marriage. I don't want you tied to me when you don't have to be. You should be able to live your life, have fun, pick and choose who you want to be with. I wanted you to have the kind of freedom that was robbed from you in Cuba."

"Wanted?" Lyla whispered.

Case sighed. "Wanted. Want. Meeting you again has muddled the water somewhat. It would have been better if we had not met each other now."

"I don't think so." Lyla had a smile in her voice, "I think we met at the right time, both times."

Case nodded. "Maybe my island girl, who knows."

Chapter Seven

His island girl. Lyla closed her eyes and willed the sleep to come. Case Wiley had called her his island girl. They had talked after that, but when he said island girl it stuck her in head.

Jules had returned with details of a video shoot, and she had excused herself. It was a long day and she should feel sleepy, but she was curiously awake.

She had too many things on her mind. There was the Case thing. His talk about setting her free had struck a chord. She didn't want that. She wanted to get to know him better and for them to have a proper wedding and marriage and live happily ever after.

She curled up on her side and stared at the curtains fluttering in the night breeze. She had turned off the AC and opened the patio doors. She had always been fanciful especially as a child. When she was about six or seven, she had become obsessed with having a father.

Just like the Alvarez family next door. Senor Alvarez had been an exceptional father figure. He was patient and kind and gentle with his children, and her as well, even though she was just the neighbor who would crouch beside his apartment door waiting for someone to open it and let her in.

That summer it had seemed as if it rained every single day in Havana. Consuela's Canadian boyfriend, Jeff, had been firmly ensconced in the one-bedroom apartment drinking Havana Club rum and smoking cigars. Because of Consuela's constant fussing over him and the cloud of smoke in the air, she had spent most of her time in the hallway near the Alvarez door.

One particular day she had seen Senor Alvarez as he entered the apartment. His children Luciana and Martina had rushed to greet him. He was a doctor, but he supplemented his income by teaching private English classes. She had developed a fantasy that he was her father. And she had unwisely started badgering Consuela about her father.

"Your father was a stupid boy who didn't have two dimes to rub together. He couldn't afford to take care of you. Forget about him. He is not important. You have me." Consuela had snarled. "Now get out, Jeff and I are going to do adult stuff. I'll call you back inside when we are through."

But she hadn't been satisfied with the response, and she had let Consuela know. She had been thoroughly beaten and then kicked into the hallway. That was when the Alvarez family had taken pity on her and kept her with them. Even when Consuela didn't kick her out, Lyla went to their apartment. Everyone thought the main attraction had been Luciana and Martina, but it had really been their relationship to their parents, especially their father. She had wanted it as well.

And obviously the fancifulness had not dissipated, she was still yearning over something that she could not have.

Case had a relationship. Case wanted to marry someone else for real this time.

It felt a bit like her impossible yearnings from childhood. She got up out of bed and pushed her hair from her face. She was thirsty. The dinner was good but very spicy, and that rum cake was as rich as any dessert she had ever had.

She pulled on her slippers and headed downstairs. The night lights came on automatically when she walked down the stairs illuminating her way. She glanced at the clock in the living room. It was seven minutes after two.

She headed to the kitchen and stopped abruptly. Case was sitting at the island and looking at his phone.

"Oh hey," She whispered.

"Hey," Case glanced at her and then widened his eyes.

She looked down at herself. She was in sleeping shorts and a tube top. It was pretty decent, much more modest than what people wore on the road, or at least that is what she told herself as she self-consciously headed to the refrigerator and removed a bottle of water.

"I got thirsty."

"I can't sleep." Case murmured. "I probably slept too much today."

She unscrewed the cap from the bottle and nodded. "You did sleep a lot."

"So what's keeping you up?" Case asked. He looked down at his phone at the same time and missed her expression.

She was happy that he did because she was staring at him like a love-struck fan. The fade cut that he had suited him. He had been running his fingers through the curly top. It was adorably tousled.

"I er…I was thinking about the mother and the father thing," She said searching for something, anything to say because she was fixated on the errant curl that was on his forehead.

Case looked up. "I knew it would affect you. It would affect me too, knowing that my mother was really my grandmother and that who I thought was my sister was really my mother. It's mind-boggling when you think about it. Have you ever met Valentina?"

"No." Lyla sat in a chair beside him. "Consuela didn't talk about her. I just knew that she sent money every month. If she missed the payments, Consuela might call her names, and I'd get treated especially badly that month. Now I know why."

"Now you know," Case murmured. "Sorry to break it to you so casually at dinner. I usually have more tact."

"It was okay. I am fine. I had Sienna for five whole years." Lyla sipped her water contemplatively. "I am happy that I got the opportunity to get out of the situation in Cuba and I feel more than blessed that I got some time with one of the best women on the planet."

"She was one of a kind." Case sighed. "Her death hit me hard. You know when Jules took you home the day after Cuba. She hugged me, and she had tears in her eyes. She said, I dreamed this Case, I love this little girl already, thank you for taking her home to me."

"Sienna was a dreamer." Lyla blinked back tears. "She said it was in the Bible that in the last days sons and daughters will prophesy, young men, will see visions and old men dream dreams."

"Except she wasn't an old man." Case chuckled.

Lyla joined him. She liked to hear him laugh. Who was she kidding, she liked everything about him. She took a sip of her water and then covered it, "I should go back to bed to count sheep."

"I count music notes." Case smiled. "I dissect it break it

down until I drift off."

"I am a business major who never learned music. I should try to recall economic theories. Keynesian, Monetarism… can't even remember the rest."

"Or you could stay for a while longer and tell me about you," Case said huskily. "We are both awake."

Lyla nodded and sat down. "What do you want to know about me?"

Case looked at her. "Everything. Your likes, dislikes, what makes you happy."

Lyla gave him a mock frown. "You will have to return the favor."

"I will." Case grinned. "I am so uncomplicated you are going to find me boring."

"Never," Lyla responded passionately and then she cleared her throat. "You know, I never thanked you for rescuing me."

She looked at him with a mixture of adoration and hero worship.

Case nodded. "You are welcome. I should thank you too."

"Why?" Lyla asked. "I didn't do anything for you."

"You were my opportunity to help." Case smiled contemplatively. "The giver of a gift is more blessed than the receiver, especially if no strings are attached. Every opportunity to help is a blessing. You can pay it forward, and that will be reward enough. I love giving, and I expect nothing in return."

"I know." Lyla shook her head. "I don't know anybody like you."

"There are plenty of people like me. All of my brothers are like that." Case chuckled. "It's the Joseph Wiley genes. My father was like that too. And my mom. And most of the people we grew up with. Old country folks. Everyday people. They might not have the resources to do much, but they help where they can."

"Does your girlfriend know about me?" Lyla asked, "I mean that you have a wife?"

"No." Case grimaced. "I will have to tell her. I think she'll understand though. She's into helping people too. She's a minister."

"A minister, as in pastor?" Lyla widened her eyes. "Really?"

"Yes." Case nodded. "We met while I was at her church. They call it a ministry. She's the head pastor."

"Oh," Lyla raised an eyebrow. "She is older than you?"

Case nodded. "Yes, but I don't care about that."

"Age doesn't matter. Romance doesn't matter. Love doesn't matter." Lyla smirked, "You are strange."

"Maybe I am." Case winked. "But I think love matters. It's just that I don't want to ever lose myself in it. I never want to lose my head or heart over a woman. Courtship, marriage should be approached sensibly."

Lyla grinned. "You know people would look at you and assume that you are a player with a million groupies in every port. I am sure women lose their minds and hearts over you all the time."

Case laughed. "I have gotten some really 'out there' fan mail. Many women have told me that they would like to have my babies, others have threatened suicide if I don't return the love."

"Can you imagine if you did R & B?" Lyla mused. "Or performed on stage with your shirt off? My goodness. They would blow up your posters and have lewd, lustful fantasies."

"I could pose like this." Case ran his fingers through his hair and gave her a come-hither smile.

Lyla gasped. "You shouldn't do that."

Case smiled. "Okay, okay. I don't want to cause anyone to lust."

"I don't think you can help it. You don't know the power of your smile or the way you look at people." Lyla grumbled. "I went to your concert, and I swear you were looking straight at me. I almost swooned with the hundreds of women around me. You should perform with a paper bag over your head."

Case laughed and hit the counter. "It's just genetics, Lyla. I had nothing to do with it. Like you have nothing to do with yours."

"I am sure your fiancée is not comfortable with so many women wanting you," Lyla smirked. "And she'll be extremely disappointed to hear that you are already married. You might not know this, but women are possessive and jealous, whether they say it or not."

"She's not possessive or jealous." Case frowned. "If she were, I wouldn't ask her to marry me. She is too busy for jealousy. I like it just like that. Besides, she knows she has nothing to worry about. I am not into fleeting sexual relationships with strange women who like me for my looks or my voice or my money, women who can't bother to know me intimately. I can't be bothered with the women who just like the image."

"Intimate is hard." Lyla nodded. "Many of us don't even want to know ourselves intimately much less another person."

"That's so true." Case gave her a half smile and then changed the subject. "Now tell me about you, Island Girl. How did you adjust when you first lived with Sienna?"

"It was easy," Lyla grimaced, "she spoke Spanish, and I was eager to learn English."

"And now you barely have an accent." Case murmured. "Amazing."

"Sienna was amazing," Lyla murmured. "I didn't know what having a mother was really like until she came into my life. When I lived with Consuela, it was one boyfriend after another, sometimes she forgot that I was around, but with Sienna, I finally felt loved and wanted. She showed me how it could be."

"So leaving you with her was a good decision then?" Case nodded. "That's a relief."

"It was the best decision." Lyla blinked back tears. "I remember the first time we went shopping for clothes. I told her that my favorite color was verde oscuro, dark green like the green of the forest. I didn't know much English at the time to explain that the green I was talking about was not just plain green. Oh boy! She went hog wild with the greens, neon, teal, you name it she bought it. Sienna is the reason I don't wear green anymore. I don't have one piece of green in my wardrobe."

Case laughed. "She spoiled it for you?"

"Oh yes," Lyla chuckled, "I learned pretty early that if I liked something, I couldn't let Sienna know or she would shower me with it."

"What else did she kill for you?" Case asked.

"Pudding. Sweet potato pudding." Lyla grimaced, "Cuban food. She bought a Cuban cookbook and experimented every day. I ended up begging her to let me get familiar with some Jamaican food, and I told her I would cook from then on. Sienna was many things, but a good cook was not one of them."

Case chuckled. "So what do you do for fun?"

Lyla drummed her fingers on the table. "Let's see, I like the beach. I like hiking. I like to go to new places, and I love concerts."

"Those are similar to what I like." Case steepled his fingers under his chin. "I love hiking more than the beach though. I love to hike in the mountains. There is something humbling about trying to conquer a tall mountain. It makes you feel small and God great."

"Yes!" Lyla nodded, "that's a part of it."

"I love going to new places too. Wherever I tour I try to take in a site or two."

"I sometimes imagine what that is like and I envy you a little bit." Lyla twirled a hair around her finger.

Case smiled. "Sometimes it's fun, like this week. The schedule is not heavy. I have a single to promote but it's practically promoting itself, and top artists are covering it. It is getting heavy rotation on the airwaves. People know the words to the lyrics when I go to concerts. I have been blessed."

"And what do you like?" Lyla asked. She was staring at him intently with laser-sharp focus, her eyes not wavering from his.

When he stared back, he could feel the tension between them. The air fairly crackled with it. It was on the tip of his tongue to say—you. I like you. Totally and completely. One look since we met, and I am a goner. I have not been the same since.

He cleared his throat instead, but for the life of him, he couldn't remember what he liked apart from her. This was alarming; this was the madness he scoffed at in the past.

"Music." He finally said in the silence that Lyla did nothing to break. "My life is all about the music, and I like all genres, classical, reggae. You name it, I like it."

Lyla smiled, her bow-shaped lips stretching across her teeth in the most beguiling way. "I knew you would say that. I meant what's your favorite stuff, color and that kind of thing."

"Oh," Case dragged his mind from her lips and concentrated on his favorite stuff. "I er…I guess I like red, and black, white and grey. Fish is my favorite food as you heard. My hobby is my job--playing music, writing lyrics and music, performing. I guess when I think about it, I am boring."

Lyla laughed. "No, you are not."

"Yes I am," Case sighed, "I need to broaden my focus, maybe I should take up knitting."

Lyla laughed, a genuine loud laugh that she had to clap her hand over her mouth to stifle the noise.

Case laughed with her as well.

"I can't imagine you knitting." Lyla wiped her eyes. "I just can't."

"I can see it, sitting in a rocking chair, Ferb at my feet while I knit and watch the soaps on television and Phineas watching me in judgmental disbelief."

"Ferb and Phineas are your cats?" Lyla choked out.

"Yep," Case chuckled. "My brothers and I share a townhouse complex, so when I am gone, they are everybody's cat. My sister-in-law, Aisha, has taken a shine to Ferb, and he is hanging out more with her these days than anyone else, but when I am home, he comes home to me. Phineas lives everywhere. Here is a picture of them, loyal to a fault. Sweetest cats on the planet."

"I like cats. Lyla took his phone and gushed over them. "I had a street cat friend in Cuba; I named him Blanco."

"Let me guess, he was white?" Case chuckled.

"Sounds better than Ferb," Lyla snickered. "Ferb Wiley sounds so strange."

"Haven't you heard of Phineas and Ferb? The cartoon?" Case widened his eyes. "They were stepbrothers from a blended family. Ferb was the one of action, and he barely speaks. I thought my cat didn't know how to meow when I rescued him as a kitten; that's why I called him Ferb."

"Never watched cartoons." Lyla chuckled. "But I

understand now."

She handed the phone back him, and their fingers touched and just like that the atmosphere changed again.

"Why did you use the name Wiley?" Case asked after another charge filled pause.

"Because I wanted to," Lyla said huskily. "I felt closer to you, and unlike Ferb Wiley, Lyla Wiley sounds good to me."

Case chuckled. "I hear you."

"Tell me about your brothers." Lyla took a sip of water. "You seem close to them."

"My brothers." Case drummed his fingers on the table. "First there is Preston, the oldest, he is the responsible one, the serious one."

"The one I am going to work for." Lyla shuddered, "I hope he is not too hard on me."

"Nah," Case grinned. "He is a fair boss. His employees love him and his family love him. He is married to Sheryl, and they have two children, Peter and Petra."

"Then there is Jordan, the second brother, who mysteriously looks like Preston, you'll find it fascinating, many people seem to be puzzled by it."

"Why?" Lyla played with a tendril of her hair near her breast and Case almost forgot what they were talking about.

"Because they ah, don't have the same mother," Case said huskily. "And they are just two months apart in age. They could be twins. Jordan is friendly and caring and slightly less of a mother hen than Preston. He is married to Shawn, and they have one girl, my outrageously frank niece, Courtney. She is four going on forty."

"I see." Lyla followed his gaze to her hand and then dropped it.

"You sound like you have a soft spot for her."

"I love all my nieces and nephew. Well, there are only

three so far, but this year is going to be a busy year. Nearly all my sisters-in-law are pregnant. Shawn, Jordan's wife, is due in November, Aisha, Walters wife is due in December, and Sandy, Saint's wife any day now."

"Your brothers have been busy." Lyla chuckled. "Tell me about the others. I want a visual in my head."

"Walter is the third brother; he is the fun one. He will use any occasion as an excuse to have a party."

"I'd like to know him." Lyla chuckled.

"You will. He is the vice president of the Wiley Group, Preston's second in command. Though they have opposite personalities, they work well together. And then there is Guy. We resemble each other more than the others. He is shorter by one inch though," Case chuckled. "I am six one. He is just six."

"Just six." Lyla giggled. "I bet you rub that in."

"Yes. Every time." Case chuckled. "He is a certified genius and a dedicated farmer who loves his own company and of course Lucia's more than anything else."

"Lucia?" Lyla asked, "Who is that?"

"His wife." Case smiled. "She is a cool girl. They were made for each other."

"Said the non-romantic," Lyla murmured.

"I didn't say it can't happen for other people." Case smirked, "all my brothers are married and happy."

"All the Wiley brothers are married, full stop." Lyla got up and kissed him fleetingly on the cheek. "Maybe we need to work on you being happy. Goodnight Case."

"Goodnight." Case looked after her bemusedly, touching the area where she had kissed.

****

It was three o'clock. Case looked on his phone and sighed.

He was too keyed up to sleep. He found the villas' exercise room which was at the back of the place and near the pool house where he assumed Shannon was staying. He kept the doors closed because he didn't want to disturb her.

He assumed that it was unusual for guests to be up and about so early in the day.

He turned on the big screen television mounted before the state-of-the-art treadmill. It had a hiking feature. He pressed the option to choose a trail.

He chose advanced and began to a virtually walk on the Inca Trail to Machu Pacchu. He turned on the television, and it was already on the sports channel. Reruns from a cricket match from the day before was on. The highlights were exciting. It kept him from thinking about the fact that he was attracted to Lyla.

Well not attracted exactly more like bewitched, captivated, beguiled, spellbound, dazzled... he ran out of synonyms, and he was not going to be thinking about it, Mount Machu Pacchu was kicking his butt, the cricket match was interesting and left no room for Lyla in his thoughts.

But her lips, they looked so soft, and she had a way to bite them when she was thinking of something. She wasn't aware of it, but he was. Oh, he was.

He had learned too much about her tonight, and it had disturbed him and disturbed his peace of mind.

Things that he shouldn't know. He now knew.

And he wasn't so gung-ho now to annul their marriage if he were to be honest with himself.

"What are you doing up?" Jules startled him in mid-thought. He yawned and blinked at Case blearily.

"Trying not to think." Case lowered the volume on the television and pointed at the clock. "What are you doing up?"

"Came to get some water and decided to investigate when I saw the light on." Jules murmured. He sat down on one of the benches and then stretched. "I should have known you would have found the gym."

Case stopped the treadmill and stretched. "I slept through the day, and it threw me off."

"Understandable." Jules slapped his palm in the middle of his forehead. "I clean forgot. Fifi Daniels is going to be present at the Gospel Fest, and I told her she could stay here. She will be here on Wednesday."

Case was in mid-stretch, and he stopped. "Say what?"

"Your fiancée…" Jules said patiently.

"She didn't say anything to me." Case frowned. "You didn't say anything to me."

"I forgot." Jules got up and saluted him. "I for one am looking forward to the drama that is about to ensue. Your wife and your fiancée under the same roof."

"For goodness sake." Case folded his arms and glared at Jules. "You are supposed to be looking out for me."

"And that is why I eagerly invited Fifi. I never met her properly or interacted with her before. Seeing someone preach on television is not the same. I want to see her without the cameras rolling. You seem to like her. I want to like her too."

Case sighed. "But Lyla is here."

"That shouldn't pose a problem. Lyla is just a girl you married for expediency. She understands her place in your life is temporary. It should be interesting to see how Fifi handles this."

Case opened his mouth to protest but he saw Jules' sly expression and closed it. He didn't like to hear the words Lyla and temporary in the same sentence.

"You are so obvious," he muttered instead. "You want a

soap opera, so you think you are just going to throw all the players in the same house and see how it plays out."

"That's right," Jules walked toward the gym door. "I think I missed my calling. I should be a movie director."

Case sat down hard on the treadmill and ran his fingers through his curls. He had a feeling his previously ordered life was going to take a major hit.

What was he going to tell Fifi? Why did he feel guilty all of a sudden?

He knew he had to tell Fifi about Lyla, but never before had he been so unsure about his feelings. He closed his eyes and thought about Fifi and what he felt, he had to hang on to that because Lyla had unwittingly thrown all of that in peril, he forced himself to remember.

Two years before…

He was hoarse. Not ordinary hoarse, the kind of hoarse where he could barely talk much less sing, and Jules had booked him for a Hope Ministries concert with thousands of people and mega gospel stars which would be televised.

"It means you have arrived." Jules had said rubbing his hands together gleefully, "They didn't even blink at your fee, and they are recording this for a live concert CD. Proceeds will go to charity."

Then Jules had gotten the phone call about Sienna being in the hospital, and he had left him in Miami. He had gone to Hope Ministries with his band to practice before the big day, and while they were setting up, he had found himself walking around. It was a huge place with modern architecture. The concert was going to be held in the main worship hall which could comfortably seat five thousand.

He had walked through the busy hallway with its fresh

flowers and mosaic tiles, and suddenly he had felt lost. Sienna's sickness was weighing on his mind. He was tired and feeling a little worse for wear, and they were going to record him live when his voice was probably at its worst.

He wandered far down the halls of Hope Ministry even meeting a tour group of youngsters as a perky guide took them through the history of the place.

Hope Ministries was founded by Bishop Garnett Daniels. It was decided by Bishop Daniels not to call this a church because our main focus is helping others, to minister. We minister to the physical, emotional, mental, vocational, and financial needs of others. Jesus did, and so should we! Don't you think?

Case watched as several persons nodded eagerly. He veered to the left and entered a courtyard that had trees, benches and a waterfall.

He sat on one of the nearest benches and started humming. Genuinely afraid that his voice was going to let him down. That's when he saw her, she was three benches over from him, inhaling and exhaling. Something about her struck a chord. She was rubbing the back of her neck and making motions to loosen up her shoulders.

And then he saw that she was on the phone.

And then he heard snippets of the conversation, "Cory Daniels was never close to the Bishop, he wasn't his first choice to run this place, he just left the seminary. Surely he couldn't convince two-thirds well thinking people that he can run this place."

She got up and started pacing, walking by him and almost yelling at the person on the phone.

"I don't need to do anything to prove myself to anyone. The Bishop died three months ago, and already the hyenas are out for blood. This is ridiculous. I don't know if I am working with Christians or politicians!"

Case tried not to overhear the conversation, but her voice had a desperate quality to it. She was an attractive woman medium built, her arms were lean and toned as if she worked out. Her skin was glowing with health. He didn't know if she had on makeup. If she did, it was artfully applied.

She made eye contact with him, and he saw that her eyes were an interesting shade of brown, russet brown eyes, they matched the streaks at the front of her hair.

She was in mid-sentence when she became aware that he was sitting there. She did a double take and then hung up the phone.

"My goodness, you are good looking, aren't you?" She breathed, and then laughed and walked over to him with her hand outstretched. "Hello, I am Fifi Daniels."

He shook her hand. "I am Case Wiley."

"The singer?" She grinned. "I am most looking forward to hearing you tonight."

"And I am worried that I can't perform." Case grimaced and then cleared his throat. "My voice is not a hundred."

"It is nothing that Jesus can't fix." Fifi winked at him. "Want us to pray about it? I am supposed to be leading out with a prayer session right now for the success of tonight. Let us pre-empt them."

"I'll never refuse prayer," Case had quipped.

She held his hand, said a heartfelt prayer and then kissed him on his cheek.

"You'll get better for tonight," she said with certainty. "I believe it. You should too."

She had squeezed his hand and then walked away.

He had later found out that she was 'the' Fifi Daniels, the young widow of the late Bishop Daniels. She was the current head of the ministry and apparently a miracle worker. His throat had felt as good as new when he performed, and she was in the wings to greet him.

"I told you." She had grinned. "You are an anointed singer."

"And you are an anointed preacher." He had responded with a grin. She could bring her points across and captivate a crowd, he had fallen in love with her presence, the way she captivated a stage. Her eloquent speech, her way with words. He had been quite literally impressed by Bishop Fifi Daniels.

On his way out she had given him her number. She wanted him to come and sing for her ministry again.

He had done so. He liked Fifi. She was a genuine person. She was easy to talk to and was a good listener. It was in one of their conversations that she had mentioned the conversation that he had overheard in the atrium.

"My stepson is out to get me," Fifi had said helplessly. "He is working here now and trying to campaign to get the board on his side. They are buying into the madness that only a fellow Daniels and a male can run this place successfully."

"That sucks." Case remembered saying.

"And I am going to Africa. Plans were in place long before the little runt came on the scene. Who knows what he will get up to when I am away? Fifi said, come with me, Case, please. It would mean a lot. It would make headlines, trust me. Even Cory couldn't top that."

"I can't go to Africa. I am fully booked for the next couple of months. Can he top an engagement?" Case had asked flippantly. "I mean if we get married, there is no way that he can squeeze you out of your post there. Evangelist Fifi Wiley, wife of the singer C. Wiley has a nice ring to it."

"That's not a good reason to get married." Fifi had said faintly. "But yes, I accept. That's brilliant! I bet Cory will cool down when I tell him that."

"I hope he does. It's nothing," Case said, "I like you. I like you a lot, Fifi. We could make it work."

Case opened his eyes and looked around. But here he was in Barbados, the foolishness of youth had caught up with him, and he realized that he felt a different kind of feeling for Lyla. It wasn't lofty and ideal and filled with admiration. He wanted to go upstairs invite her to his room and consummate their marriage.

He couldn't believe when he had seen her earlier in her boy shorts and her tight shirt. He hoped that wasn't how she dressed normally because it was indecent, and he couldn't think about anything else.

He closed his eyes and swallowed. He was a man. This was as far away from admiration and a crush. This was attraction. Deep attraction. The kind of attraction that he had never experienced before. The longer he was exposed to her. Maybe he should be thankful that Fifi was coming by, maybe that would put a buffer on these outrageous feelings. He had never thought of Fifi like that, and he had asked her to get married.

He got up and went back on the treadmill for another bout of hiking.

Chapter Eight

Case was avoiding her. Lyla could figure out that much by the Wednesday of her three days in Barbados. It was true that Jules had assigned him to do several promotions and he was busy, but it was pretty obvious that he was keeping out of her way. It was also obvious that Jules was equally determined to entertain them.

The first day they had all gone on a private Catamaran cruise in the evening, it was supposed to coincide with sunset.

It was beautiful. Case and Jules had gone snorkeling, and then they had dinner on the cruise and even then, Case had kept his distance. He avoided looking at her or talking to her directly.

On day two, Jules and Case spent most of the day at radio and television stations and she and Brandi lounged around the house. In the evening they ate dinner alone because Case was invited to a Gospel Fest event and Jules had a business meeting.

Day three, Jules arranged for them to do a half day tour. He called a taxi, and they were heading out the door when Case was coming in from running. He had seen them leaving and their eyes had met. He had barely given them a nod.

Brandi had commented on it then. "What's up with Case?"

She didn't know. What had gone wrong? Was it something she did?

Brandi had dropped the topic, and they had done their half day tour with about twenty other tourists, so there was no privacy to talk. They visited Harrison's Cave, and she was still floored by the beauty of the place. It was her first time going into a cave, and she was awed. She was finding out for the first time about stalagmites and stalactites, and she was positively floored when she saw that there were pools and waterfalls underground.

She hadn't quite recovered from that when they stopped at Hunte Garden's, and she saw plants that she had never known existed. And then to end the assault on her senses, they stopped at Bathsheba Beach, named after the wife of King David.

Brandi was on her phone talking to Adam when she looked over at Lyla. "I don't know what is going on with Lyla and Case, they are estranged. Apart from that we are having a blast of a time."

After she hung up, she turned to Lyla. "What did you do to Case, Lyla?" Brandi asked loudly as if she was hard of hearing.

Even the taxi man looked back at them in the back seat.

"Nothing." Lyla snapped at Brandi. "Nothing at all."

She looked at Brandi repentantly, "sorry for snapping. I am hungry."

Brandi fanned her off. "No need to be sorry. I am hungry

too. We should have stopped at that local restaurant near the taxi stand. It smelled yummy."

Lyla nodded.

"Back to your situation," Brandi pursued the previous conversation. "You must have done something. Even Jules is acting suspiciously."

Lyla grimaced. "We talked the first night. It was good, lovely. I thought we were well on the way to getting to know each other and then...I don't know. We went on the cruise and then, today..."

"It's weird." Brandi shook her head. "Unless he has feelings for you and he is trying to avoid facing them. Men are like that you know, irrational."

The taxi driver looked back at them and laughed.

Lyla was relieved when he pulled up at the house. She was also a little curious because he pulled in behind another taxi.

A woman got out. Her profile looked familiar. Her hair was in a top knot, and she had on large sunglasses that covered most of her face.

"Is today the video shoot?" Brandi whispered when they got out of the car.

"No. It's tomorrow," Lyla murmured. "Remember Jules said you could be involved."

"Oh yeah." Brandi grinned. "So who is she?"

The lady turned and looked right at them and then slowly removed her glasses.

She smiled slightly and nodded.

They nodded back and headed into the house behind the driver who was carrying her bags.

She followed. Lyla looked at Brandi with apprehension. The lady made her uncomfortable. Neither Case or Jules had mentioned that they were going to be having another house guest.

They met in the foyer together and looked at each other awkwardly.

"Well, well, where is Case or his manager, Jules?" The lady asked.

"We have no idea." Brandi was the first to answer. "We were out touring."

"I guess I should introduce myself." She smiled. "My name is Fifi Daniels."

"The Fifi Daniels?" Brandi squealed. "You look different in person. You are shorter and younger looking. Those wigs they have you wearing on television does nothing for you."

Fifi smiled and held out her hand to Brandi. "Well thank you. And you are?"

"Brandi." Brandi gushed. "And this is Lyla."

Lyla shook her outstretched hand and nodded. "Hello."

"Lyla?" Fifi frowned. "That's a pretty name. I knew someone named Lyla…"

Shannon interrupted the introductions and offered to show Fifi to her room. An offer which she took up quite gladly. She looked back at Lyla while she was going up the stairs curiously.

Lyla held her stare. They were probably both caught up in some kind of déjà vu. The familiarity between them was palpable.

"I wonder which other famous person in the gospel world is Case going to invite to stay here?" Brandi asked a beatific smile on her face. "Do you think anybody else is coming?"

"I don't know," Lyla said absently. "Fifi looks so familiar though. I mean she feels familiar."

"Because you've seen her on television, duh." Brandi headed to the kitchen.

"No that's not it." Lyla followed, "I've never seen her program. I never wake up that early to watch it."

"Well, relax, maybe it will come to you." Brandi smiled. "Let's just bask in her famous presence for the moment. I am going to have to tell Adam this. He will flip. He loves her. His mother wrote to her program asking them to pray for her for healing and she was healed."

Lyla nodded. "So, her faith made her well not Fifi Daniels and company."

"Cynic," Brandi mumbled. "She always had faith. Hope Ministries made a difference."

"Who is a cynic?" Jules was sitting at the island in the kitchen; the phone pressed firmly to his ear.

"Lyla," Brandi grumbled and then her tone brightened. "Guess who is here? Fifi Daniels! The Fifi Daniels!"

"She is here? Already?" Jules looked at his watch, "Case won't be back for another hour or so."

"I guess she'll have to hang with us." Brandi grinned. "I can't believe it. I am going to get to hang out with Evangelist Fifi Daniels."

Jules looked at Lyla sheepishly. "So, you okay with this?"

"Why wouldn't I be?" Lyla frowned.

"Nothing." Jules shrugged. "This is not for me to get involved with."

"What are you talking about, Jules?" Lyla looked at him suspiciously. She liked Jules, but she hated when he got sly and cryptic.

"I'll let Case handle his own telling in his own time." Jules winked at her. "Did I tell you that when I lived in Cuba I had an addiction to vaca frita? I loved it. I asked Shannon if she could do it for dinner and she said no, she didn't even know what it is."

"What's a vaca frita?" Brandi asked.

Lyla rolled her eyes at the obvious change in subject and glared at Jules. "It means fried cow."

"And they used to serve it a lot in the nightclubs." Jules licked his lips. "I miss those days. Rich Cuban rum and vaca frita. I suddenly had a hankering for it today."

Brandi giggled. "Tell us more, Jules. What else did you get up to while you were in Cuba?"

"That's where I fell in love for the first time. She was a pretty Latina. Her name was Maria. She had eyes the color of dark spiced rum, lips as plump and juicy as a cherry." Jules shook his head regretfully, "unfortunately I was a man about town with an exotic buffet of ladies, and I fell in love every week, but I still remember Maria and her vaca frita. My most memorable one-night stand."

He cleared his throat, "I can almost taste it now, she served it with coconut rice."

Lyla laughed. "I could make it for you. I used to make it for myself. It's pretty easy to do."

"Would you really?" Jules looked at Lyla excitedly. "I wasn't fishing for you to make it, you know."

"If Shannon will allow me in her kitchen," Lyla headed to the freezer, "and if she has flank steak."

It turned out Shannon had flank steak and coconut cream for the coconut rice.

Shannon joined Jules and Brandi in the kitchen, and they watched Lyla work. Jules, of course, led the conversation, telling stories of his various jaunts around the world and his relationship woes.

"Do you have any children, Mr. Jules?" Shannon who was quite happy to have someone else do her job. She was quite relaxed and heavily involved in the conversation.

"No." Jules shook his head. "It was my mother's greatest wish before she died, but I had testicular cancer in my youth."

"She had me." Lyla looked up from shredding the beef.

"And that's true." Jules nodded. "She had Lyla and was

quite content with that."

He continued with his tales of grand adventurous, describing his night-time escapades in Cuba. It was the hush in the kitchen that made Lyla aware that they were joined by someone else. She had been busy over the skillet with the oil, and completely zoned out.

Cooking often did that to her, but she sensed a change in the air when she looked up, Fifi Daniels was there. She had changed into a strapless long maxi dress, and she looked fresh and well rested. She had removed the glasses; her hair was no longer in the top knot, it looked as if she had washed it. It was laying around her shoulders slightly wet.

"Something smelled good in here; I just had to come and investigate." She smiled over at Lyla and then at Jules who for once looked like he was tongue tied.

"I have never met you face to face," he said after a pause, "I am Julius Harvey."

Fifi shook his hand and then sat at the island. "Where is Case?"

"At a recording session with the festival committee." Jules had on his posh voice and had begun to talk more formally.

Shannon started going on about Fifi's program Hope For Humanity and Brandi too was in full fangirl mode.

"What are you cooking?" Fifi asked when there was a lull in the conversation. "It smells familiar."

"Vaca frita," Jules said reverently, "I requested it, Cuban food."

Fifi nodded.

"Have you ever been to Cuba?" Jules asked.

Fifi laughed. "Oh yes, I have. Have you ever been Lyla?"

Lyla looked across at her, and the sense of familiarity came back. "I was born there, lived there until I was fourteen."

She didn't know if anybody else noticed it, but Fifi Daniels looked spooked when she said that.

"How interesting," Fifi murmured. "Where in Cuba?"

Something told Lyla that this was not a casual questioning. Fifi Daniels was interested in placing her, and it was mutual.

"Havana." She answered while looking Fifi in the eye. "I lived with my mother Consuela Martinez in Havana."

"Who she recently found out was not her mother but her grandmother." Jules inserted. "Amazing isn't it?"

Fifi Daniels nodded stiffly. "That is er… amazing."

"That Consuela was something else," Jules continued, "you know she sold Lyla to Case for one hundred US dollars? Case had to marry her to rescue her."

The kitchen was silent after he said that. Shannon had her eyes opened wide looking between them as if she had just heard the most shocking news. "Mr. Case is married to Miss Lyla?"

Brandi sighed.

But it was Fifi's reaction that Lyla found most interesting. She jerked in her chair as if somebody had slapped her.

"I am so sorry," Jules looked repentant. "I forgot to mention that Fifi is engaged to Case."

Lyla gasped.

And then like a three-piece tragedy in a play everyone froze awkwardly. They heard the front door open. Case was home.

****

Jules couldn't escape the kitchen and the hash he had made of things fast enough. He suddenly remembered an urgent phone call he needed to make.

No one heard Shannon's excuse, and Brandi slowly shuffled out of the room when Case appeared.

"Hey," Fifi got up to greet him as if nothing had happened and a bombshell hadn't just dropped.

Lyla licked her lips uncomfortably. Fifi Daniels was Case's fiancée?

"Hey," Case was hugging Fifi. Lyla watched them almost forgetting to turn down the fire so that her beef didn't burn. "What's going on?"

He spoke above Fifi's head which reached him a little under his chin. "Everybody just scattered when I stepped into the room. Usually, that is not what happens."

"Your manager Julius just put his mouth in it." Fifi was the one who answered. "He declared that Lyla is your wife and I am the fiancée."

"Oh," Case widened his eyes.

"Yes, oh." Fifi moved away from Case and then sat in the chair that Jules had occupied.

"Hi Lyla," Case said awkwardly. It was impossible for him not to drink her in like a starving man without water. She was in a simple orange swirl summer dress, and she was cooking something that smelled good.

"Hey," Lyla grimaced. "I am cooking Jules' favorite Cuban dish because he had a bout of nostalgia."

"And then I came in and we started talking about Cuba, and here we are." Fifi looked between Case and Lyla. "Everyone else scurried off to avoid the catfight. Unfortunately, I am not in the mood for a fight. I quite like Lyla."

Case nodded. "I am glad to hear that. I should have told you about Lyla and the whole marriage thing before I proposed."

"It's okay." Fifi glanced at Lyla fondly. "I heard the story; I can't be mad at you for helping her."

Lyla looked at Fifi who was watching her. Her eyes were almost teary. "She is a gorgeous girl," Fifi said.

Case cleared his throat. "Yes, she is."

Lyla was confused. Why was Fifi Daniels so nice? She even called her gorgeous. It was puzzling. Any minute now she would be asking for a hug. She didn't want Fifi Daniels to be so lovely. She wanted to dislike the woman who Case was engaged to. She wasn't particularly in the mood for drama, but she had expected fireworks, not blanket acceptance and compliments.

"I want to hear more about your life in Cuba, Lyla, when you have the time," Fifi said huskily. She cleared her throat. "That's if you don't have a problem with sharing."

Lyla nodded uncertainly. "Sure. I don't have a problem with sharing. There is nothing much to tell."

Fifi got up. "Case, can we talk?"

"Yes," Case nodded. "I am guessing this conversation is long overdue."

Lyla watched them as they headed in the direction of the beach. It was deserted out there; she was sure that they would have all the privacy that they needed. She wished that she could hear what they were talking about.

Chapter Nine

Fifi was still reeling from her meeting with Lyla earlier in the day and finding out that she was Case's wife. She was also shaken by seeing Jules. She recognized him. He hadn't changed much from when she met him in Cuba.

Her mind was churning with everything she had to deal with in the last few hours. She had almost forgotten that her mission here was to convince Case that they needed to get married if he was serious about it.

That was not going to happen. Case was already married. She was going to lose her position in the ministry.

She looked across at Case. He looked pensive too. His hands were in his pockets, his posture tense. He probably thought that she was going to let him have it about Lyla, but she couldn't. She wouldn't.

She had her share of secrets and in the whole scheme of things. Him marrying a little girl to save her from that kind of life was heroic not something to be ashamed of.

"How do you feel about her?" Fifi asked when they had walked in silence some distance down the beach.

There was no one around—just the water and silence.

"Confused," Case murmured. "I just met her Saturday night. I haven't seen her since we got her out of Cuba. She was a little girl then, a scrap of a thing. I impulsively married her because I didn't want her mother to sell her to someone else. And then a couple of nights ago she came to a concert and Jules invited her and her friend to be here."

Fifi sighed. "So it finally happened for you."

"What?" Case looked over at her and Fifi couldn't help but smile. He was a beautiful man. Facially perfect. It always hit her afresh when she saw him. It was the hooded eyes or was it the caramel toned skin with the pink lips. If Case wanted to model, he would make a success of it.

She cleared her throat. "Well, I could sense the chemistry between you two. I saw the way you looked at her when you came in this evening." Fifi frowned ruefully. "A look can speak a thousand words. Your eyes were drawn to her, seeking her out, and she looks at you the same. You should pursue it."

"Said my fiancée," Case frowned. "You sound as if you are breaking up with me. You sound as if you have resigned yourself to losing out to Cory."

"And you'd be right." Fifi tucked her hair behind her ear as a gust of wind tried to pull it back. "This evening was an eye-opener. In more ways than one. I can tell you right now this day was a shocker for me in more ways than one."

"Lyla and I are not married in the true sense of the word," Case protested weakly. "I can still help you get your ministry back."

"And it still would not work." Fifi stopped him mid-sentence. "In the two years since we have known each other, cumulatively, we have seen each other less than a month."

"Because there was your Africa thing." Case pointed out.

"And your Europe tour thing." Fifi chuckled. "And we have other commitments. We have not been in a proper relationship long enough for me to even get squeamish about our age difference."

"It doesn't matter." Case shrugged. "It never did."

"I know you would say that, and yes, it didn't matter but, Case, you are married. I can't be engaged to a married man. I need a single person now, in the next few weeks."

"Lyla and I can get an annulment in a matter of weeks," Case protested. "Weeks."

"And is that truly what you want?" Fifi squinted at him. "Do you want to get an annulment?"

Case looked out at sea and then looked back at her. "I don't want a complicated dramatic relationship where…"

Fifi had never seen Case at a loss for words before. She smiled, "where you will be forced to feel. She is tying you up in knots already?"

"Ah," Case sighed. "I refuse to answer that on the grounds that it might incriminate me."

"You realize that the two of us were ridiculous when we thought we could make a marriage work on just friendship?" Fifi grinned. "I might have lied to you and myself. I want it, the whole shebang passion and friendship. And I don't want to get married either to save my spot at the top of a ministry that I poured myself into.

"I want it fair and square. I want the board to say, Fifi, you are better than Cory for this position. I want them to recognize my worth as a minister. I deserve it without the politicking and nonsense. I deserve it. Without the deception and marriage. I deserve it."

"Amen." Case chuckled. "You should give them that

speech."

"Yup, I might." Fifi chuckled. "It did my heart good though, to think that a handsome young man such as yourself, who could get anyone he wanted, was interested in me and wanted to marry me. It did my ego well to think that you found me attractive."

"I do think you are attractive," Case said quickly.

"But the truth is, finding me attractive and being attracted to me as a woman are two different things. You have an ideal in your head of what a marriage should be. I don't think I am cut out for that, I would want you to change, and then we'd be unhappy."

Case shook his head. "Really? I never knew you thought this way."

"Oh yes, I do." Fifi sighed. "It's a human thing. We want to love and be loved. You've been hiding from it for too long. One day you'll get caught. Maybe you've been caught already."

Case twisted his lips. "I thought we were compatible."

"No, we aren't. I was just safe, the female evangelist who has her head on her shoulders." Fifi inhaled. "It would be a lie, I realized after assessing our situation that I don't feel like getting married again and suppressing my true self from my husband just to fit an image.

"I have secrets, Case. Huge secrets. Pesky secrets that I need to reveal but I feel I can't. I have lived a lie for so long, it is scary to say things about myself out loud.

"Today threw me for a loop. I am still coming to grips with it. Meeting Lyla and your manager, Jules, just proved to me that either God has a weird sense of humor or the six degrees of separation theory is true."

"What exactly are you talking about?" Case frowned.

"My past, my background, my family," Fifi smiled sadly,

"who I was before I became Evangelist Fifi Daniels."

"I am listening." Case turned to face her fully. "You know I am not the judge and condemn type. You know my family background, how bad could yours be?"

"I know you are not the judgmental type." Fifi inhaled. "But it doesn't make it easier to share. As you know, I was born in Cuba as well."

Case opened his mouth and forgot to close it.

"Bet you never knew that." Fifi sighed, "my dad died when I was ten, and my mom and I lived together. We never quite had enough to get by, and my mother turned to other means to survive."

Case was not looking at her while she spoke. His attention was directed out at the sea. "You were a prostitute?"

"My mother sold me to Santiago when I was eleven." Fifi sighed, "for a grand total of twenty US dollars."

Case gasped. "What?"

"Yes, I was cheaper than Lyla. She has a beautiful name by the way. I always liked it." Fifi sighed, "luckily I had asthma. And I say luckily because I had an attack the day I was sold, so bad it put me in the hospital. I told the doctor what happened and when I got better I was placed at the orphanage. By the way, they don't call it an orphanage in Cuba. It is called casas de niños sin amparo filial; it literally means children without family protection. I had a house mother whose her name was Lyla. Hence the love for the name."

"Anyway, I was adopted the following year by a childless couple. They were very good to me. To answer your question I was never a prostitute. I was rescued just like Lyla."

"Sorry, I jumped to that conclusion," Case said contritely.

"It's okay." Fifi chuckled, "I could easily have been. There aren't many persons who were as lucky as us."

"So what's the big horrible secret about your past that you said you had?" Case asked curiously. "The pesky secret?"

"Well I…I was an exotic dancer for a while." Fifi bit her lip, "after I left my adoptive parents' home, I found my sister."

"I didn't know you had a sister." Case quirked a brow.

"I have several sisters." Fifi grimaced. "My father was married three times. My mother was the last. My sister got me a job. She worked in a nightclub."

Case chuckled. "So you were a stripper?"

"For a very short while," Fifi said hurriedly. "I would appreciate it if you never mention this to anyone, ever. It is my story to tell, and I still feel reluctant to tell it. I might do so one day but that time in my life was brief and ill-advised."

"Okay." Case smiled. "My lips are sealed."

"My other big secret, I can't have children," Fifi said abruptly. "I had a hysterectomy three years ago."

Case hunched his shoulders and turned slightly away. "I could live with that."

"I couldn't." Fifi shrugged. "I'd feel as if I was robbing you of something. I never wanted children to be honest. I am just one of those women."

Case nodded. "I see."

"Told you I wasn't the best person to think of as a marriage partner." Fifi sighed. "The wife you have already is probably better for you."

Case sighed. "I am still going to annul our marriage, whether you break up with me or not. She deserves the chance to choose whoever she wants to be in a relationship with."

"I know what you mean, that's a generous thing to do for her." Fifi looked at him feelingly, "Thank you for being a good man, Case."

"No thanks necessary," Case murmured. "I didn't do it for

the praise or because I was even thinking of being good. I was nineteen years old; she was in trouble, I helped."

"And Jules your manager, why didn't he help?" Fifi asked curiously.

"He was already married." Case shrugged. "I think it was on wife number two at the time."

"His name wasn't always Jules was it?" Fifi asked in the silence. "I seem to remember another name."

"Raphael Julius Harvey." Case chuckled. "Don't you dare call him Raphael though."

"I won't." Fifi looked at him brightly. "Are we good, Case? No ill feelings toward me?"

"No." Case shook his head. "None."

"See, I told you it would be easy," Fifi inhaled raggedly "I hope my visit to Cuba will be just as easy. I might come down to Jamaica for a week or two in the summer. Who knows? Maybe I will be out of a job. I should take a vacation and then think about starting my own ministry."

"You would still come?" Case raised an eyebrow.

"Of course, we'll remain friends." Fifi held out her hand for him to shake. "And I want to get to know Lyla too."

"Why?" Case frowned.

"Because I like her." Fifi avoided looking into his eyes. She missed the speculative gleam that appeared in his.

Chapter Ten

It was the weirdest dinner on record. Lyla felt like she was in the twilight zone. Jules had high praise for the meal, but he was mostly silent after that. He kept glancing at Fifi with avid interest.

Brandi kept prodding Lyla under the table with her feet whenever she thought something unusual was going on, which was every other minute. The nonverbal communication around the table was hot and heavy. So many conversations were being had without anyone uttering a word.

Fifi Daniels was the one who broke the heavy silence with conversation about Cuba, and it was all addressed to Lyla and not in a jealous way. She was hard to read. Lyla felt as if she were more interested in her than her fiancé. Case was mostly silent. He seemed introspective.

Except for effusive appreciation of the meal she had not heard him speak since they all sat down to have dinner.

Case was brooding over something. Lyla could imagine

all the wheels in his brain working overtime. She gave him more than one furtive glance. He held her latest one, and she looked away first, smack dab into Fifi's eyes. She was sitting beside Case directly across from Lyla.

"Who taught you how to cook, Lyla, this is good. I had forgotten how good Cuban food was. There was a restaurant near where I lived in Miami. Your vaca frita could rival theirs."

Lyla cleared her throat. "I watch Consuela make it when I was younger. It was her favorite dish along with ajiaco and tostones."

"What on earth is ajiaco and tostones?" Brandi asked.

"Ajiaco is chicken and potato soup and tostones are twice fried green plantains." Fifi was the one who answered. "I love tostones. You cut the green plantains and fry them then smash them and fry them again. Then you sprinkle them with salt."

"We do that in Jamaica," Brandi said. "My grandmother did it with half-ripe plantains though. I like it with a little sweet in it."

"Consuela liked it green," Lyla said wistfully, "when she made it you knew it was going to be a good day because she was usually in a good mood."

"Consuela, your grandmother?" Fifi asked softly.

"Yes." Lyla nodded. "I well, I grew up thinking she was my mother."

"It is hard adjusting to her not being a grandmother," Fifi said, "I understand."

Lyla nodded. "She wasn't a good parent. I used to think I had the worst mother in all of Cuba."

"How bad was she?" Fifi asked waiting for her to speak as if it mattered to her.

Lyla grimaced. It wasn't something that she wanted to talk

about with strangers. Especially Fifi Daniels, Case's super nice fiancée. Why did Fifi have to be so nice? And why was she so interested in her?

She answered the question, choosing her words carefully. "Consuela was selfish and preferred to spend time with her boyfriends. I spent most of my time with the neighbors."

Fifi winced. "You had a tough upbringing."

"That I did." Lyla nodded. "What about you?"

It was high time to turn the tables on Fifi. She was the only one answering questions about herself.

"Me?" Fifi looked at her in stunned silence.

Lyla nodded. "Yes, how did you grow up? Did you have the perfect parents?"

"No, I didn't," Fifi murmured looking cornered, "in fact my background is a lot similar to yours. I got out when I could. I walked away and just left everything behind when I got the opportunity to. In hindsight that may not have been the best thing to do. I...I..."

Jules snapped his fingers in the middle of Fifi's stumbling. "I know why you look so familiar, Fifi Daniels."

He was looking at Fifi knowingly. "You resemble a dancer at the Salsa Club in Havana, her name was Maria. Oh goodness, that girl could move, and she cooked the best vaca frita. Just the scent of it brings back memories of our one night together. No offense Lyla but she was the absolute boss at this meal."

Lyla shook her head. "None taken, Jules."

"Is she the one who you fell in love with for the first time?" Brandi chuckled.

"Yes." Jules nodded. "But she disappeared on me after our night together."

Fifi glanced furtively at Case who had stopped eating and was slowly sipping his water.

Lyla observed that he didn't look back at Fifi. Instead, he was holding himself with sudden tension.

What was going on between them? Lyla wondered. She was so lost in speculation that she almost missed Fifi's answer to Jules.

"They say people look alike and that everyone has a double in this world. We are not that genetically diverse."

Jules nodded. "I have to agree. People commented all the time that my mother looked like Lyla."

"Maybe you two should do a DNA test," Case interjected. "I mean, think about it, you were in Cuba at about the same time she was conceived."

Jules opened his eyes wide and then laughed. "Nah, I can't get a woman pregnant. I had testicular cancer. Chemo damaged my reproductive system. They wanted me to store sperm for future use if I had the mind to, but even then, my sperm count was so low. I guess I was a lost cause. Why do you think my mother was so happy to treat Lyla like a granddaughter? She knew she was the only chance she would have."

"You had chemo after Cuba." Case reminded him. "Surely there could be a slim chance that Lyla could be yours, you did run through half the female population in Havana, didn't you? Maybe your one-night stand with this exotic dancer resulted in a child."

Fifi got up from the table abruptly. "Excuse me, ladies and gentlemen. I have an early start tomorrow, and I have not even prepared my speech."

Lyla watched as she walked away.

Case didn't look back at Fifi. He wasn't acting like a man in love. In fact, he seemed as if he was intent on pushing the absurd idea that she could be related to Jules and he was taking it seriously.

Jules found it funny as well. He was the one who was looking after Fifi as she exited the kitchen as if all the hounds of hell were at her feet.

"I hope I didn't offend the sainted minister with comparing her to my one-night stand?" Jules asked concerned. "I doubt she has ever been to a night club in her life; she certainly looks a lot like Maria though."

"Now that Maria was fun. I always visit the Salsa club hoping to see her again. She could have been a keeper if she had stuck around. She would have saved me from marrying wife number one, and I would not have met wife number two."

Case sighed. "Maybe you should have a private talk with Fifi and apologize?"

"Yes, definitely," Jules grunted. "I am blaming my reminiscing on the vaca frita, it is giving me deja vu vibes."

"I think you should trust your instincts," Case said contemplatively. "It's weird huh, that your episode with Maria was approximately twenty-one years ago. About the time that Lyla was conceived."

Jules chuckled. "You are in a strange mood."

Case shrugged and then looked at her. "You finished eating, Lyla?"

"Yes," Lyla said eagerly, and then it hit her, maybe she shouldn't be so eager. Obviously, it was their turn to talk. What was he going to tell her, that Fifi had told him to annul their marriage immediately?

"Would you like to take a walk?" Case got up. "I am in the mood to stretch my legs. I was in the studio all day."

"Yes." Lyla got up slowly. The elation she had felt when he invited her to walk disappearing almost as soon as it appeared.

"I'll clean up," Brandi volunteered. "It's only fair since

you cooked. Maybe you two should carry your umbrella, it was drizzling earlier."

And there went her only legitimate excuse.

"I should go get my shoes," Lyla said.

****

It started raining as soon as they stepped outside. Case laughed. He was in a strange mood tonight because he was almost afraid to trust his thoughts.

What he was thinking was fantastic, fanciful, bizarre and couldn't be true.

He could do with a good old fashion rain thrashing. He hadn't walked in the rain since he was a boy living in Portland and he couldn't ask Lyla to walk in the rain with him.

He wasn't much in the mood for conversation either. He didn't know why he asked her to come with him. Maybe he just wanted her close. The past two days had been a study in agony as he forced himself to stay away from her.

He looked at her to say that they shouldn't bother, that he would go alone, but she had her head up to the sky with her arms outstretched.

"I love this. The water feels just right."

"Okay then. A rainy walk it is," Case said, liking her attitude.

They walked without talking for a while. Lyla was quite happy to try to capture raindrops with her tongue. They took the beach road. Traffic was light. A lady walked her dog and bid them a pleasant evening.

Case smiled. There were other people like them who loved walking in the rain and thought nothing of it. A car came careening down the road, and he held Lyla's hand pulling her close to him. Though they were walking on the sidewalk, it was an automatic protectiveness. Something he realized that he had for her.

He didn't release her hand after that. It felt natural to hold it. She must have thought the same; she curled her fingers around his.

And then the rain came down in earnest. He stopped her before they left side street and reached the highway intersection.

"Do you want us to go back?" Case looked down the road; they had walked a good distance, each of them lost in their thoughts. They were holding hands as if it were the most natural thing to do.

They stood under the glare of the condo lights. Lyla looked at him water was dripping down her face; her hair had formed into wet clumps of curls that snaked along her cheekbone and down her blouse front. She licked her lips as they stared at each other.

"Do you want to?" She asked, her voice husky.

But Case wasn't sure they were talking about heading back to the villa. He heard in her voice a question for the future.

Did he want to go back to the way they were? That was kind of impossible now. He knew her, talked to her, liked her, was holding her hands. That was a first step.

"Case?" Lyla asked softly.

He tightened his fingers around hers. "What do you want?"

"I want to hang with you for as long as I can." Lyla smiled. "I don't know if I'll get this opportunity again."

He exhaled to ease the tension in his head. "I'll be in Jamaica this summer, most of the summer, we can hang out again. As often as you want."

"Just as friends?" Lyla asked cautiously.

"We can get to know each other." Case laced his fingers with hers.

"And what about Fifi?" Lyla asked. "Are you still planning to marry her after our annulment?"

"No." Case grimaced. "She broke up with me. I am not what she wants. She wants a single man and fast."

Lyla giggled partly in relief and partly because Case's facial expression was comical. He wasn't taking the break up seriously nor did he seem broken hearted about it.

"I am not good at romance." He bemoaned. "Or love."

"Maybe you shouldn't think of romance in terms of grand gestures. Each person gives and receives love differently. I read that this love thing is simple, you find out what the persons love language is and then speak to them like that."

Case grinned. "This sounds familiar. My brother Guy gave me a book about this."

"Was it the Five Love Languages by Gary Chapman?"

"Yes," Case nodded. "Something like that."

"Did you read it?" Lyla asked.

"No." Case frowned. "My sister-in-law Lucia was reading it to me one night. I asked her to read me a bedtime story. I went up to their farm, and I was unable to sleep though I was tired. I must have picked up something subconsciously."

"You should read it." Lyla smiled.

"And that will make me a romantic person?" Case asked, "I will be fit for the real world after reading it?"

"Nah," Lyla chuckled. "It will help you to speak the love language of the people around you and those you care about. It will make you a better friend, a better brother, a better potential fiancé for some lucky girl."

"Mmm." Case brought her hand up to his lips and kissed it. "Okay."

"That is why it is good to be friends with your loved ones so that you can speak their language and they can more accurately speak yours."

"I hear you." Case nodded. "That is a piece of very friendly advice to give."

Lyla chuckled.

"I have a lot of things to chew over," Case said. "Let's go back and get out of the rain. I think we've had enough for the evening."

He held her hand all the way too. And like before, they walked without saying much but curiously it felt fine.

****

Jules woke up at his usual time, five o'clock in the morning. He had spent most of the night hearing the Carlos Santana song Maria Maria playing in his head. He had not actively thought about her in years, and now suddenly she was in his head.

Maybe that was why Fifi Daniel's had troubled him during the years. It was her similarity to Maria. He wished now he had gotten her surname, but being with exotic dancers, he hadn't been thinking about surnames at the time.

He passed bags in the hallway. And blinked his eyes at that. Who could be leaving?

It wasn't Lyla or Brandi and definitely wasn't Case. His concert was on the weekend, and the music video was today.

And it couldn't be Fifi Daniels'. Surely, she wasn't planning to just spend a single night. He thought he would have more time to talk with her, to explore his feelings of familiarity.

He found her in the kitchen clutching a cup of what looked like tea. She was lost in thought.

He looked at her profile in consternation. The sensation that she was familiar came back full blown. The line of the song, Maria, came back to him, Maria you know you're my lover

When the wind blows, I can feel you, Through the weather and even when we're apart still feels like we're together.

"Morning," Jules said in what he thought what was a pleasant voice.

She looked up at him and frowned fiercely. "Good morning Julius."

"Jules, please. My full name is Raphael Julius Harvey. I hated both my first and second names. I used to go by Raph and RJ, but I have since settled with Jules. I can live with Jules."

"Oh," she blinked rapidly at his long explanation. "Raphael is such a nice name."

"Say it in a thick Spanish accent, and I can almost imagine that you are Maria," Jules said wistfully.

She started frowning at him again.

"Are those your bags by the door?" He yawned. He didn't know why him mentioning Maria warranted such displeasure.

"Yes." Fifi nodded. "My speech is at ten, and then I am out of here."

"I thought you would stick around," Jules shrugged, "at least for Case. You two hardly see each other as it is. It is the oddest relationship."

"We are good friends, that's all." Fifi sighed. "We called off the engagement and any relationship that we may have had, but we are still friends."

"Good." Jules grinned, "I mean sorry. Case doesn't seem cut up by it. I saw him when he came in with Lyla last night. He seems like a man that has already moved on."

Fifi nodded. "I wish him the absolute best with her, if that is God's will for his life."

"Sorry about comparing you to Maria." Jules looked at her with new respect.

"That's okay. I hope she was gorgeous."

"Oh yes," Jules murmured. "Very. Just look at yourself in the mirror and then add thick curly hair. She had the same upturned nose; full wide lips and your ears are shaped the same."

"My ears?" Fifi chuckled.

"Yes, I have an ear thing." Jules winked. "She danced like a dream. It hypnotized me. Do you have relatives in Cuba? You might be related to her."

"I have relatives in Cuba," Fifi said abruptly. "I am from Cuba actually. Not all of us are related, you know. Our island is ten times bigger than yours with four times the population."

"I know," Jules said sheepishly. "It's crazy to think it. People look alike, and the truth is you give me Maria vibes."

"People look alike, like your mother and Lyla." Fifi drummed her fingers on the table, "Maybe you should do the DNA test as Case suggested."

"It was a preposterous suggestion." Jules shrugged. "I don't know Lyla's mother, Consuela or Valentina or whoever her mother is."

"It can't hurt to know though," Fifi inhaled and then got up, "since you were a man about town as Case said. My taxi should be here soon. It was nice to see you face to face, Raphael. I mean Jules. Case surely talks about you a lot."

"Likewise." Jules looked at her for a long while and then felt compelled to ask. "When will I see you again?"

"Summer. Maybe. I'll probably be out of a job then. I just heard from my friend Esme. She was urging me to tell her that Case and I tied the knot on the beach last night."

"Why the urgency?" Jules asked.

"Because I am a woman." Fifi growled, "and my late husband's son is a man because of that he apparently can run a ministry better than I can."

"I am free," Jules said jokingly, "I might not be a big name like Case, but I know many more people like him, I work with them, produce some of their stuff, manage them…"

Fifi laughed and then wiped her eyes. "Oh, Jules. Thank you for the offer but like I told Case last night, marrying to secure my position is not girl power. I might have to start my own thing. If it comes to that, I will."

"Then you need to give me a call." Jules smiled. "I can help."

Fifi fished in her bag and removed a business card and handed it to him. "Call me. We'll talk."

Jules took the card from her and immediately memorized the number. He would call her. He needed to explore further why seeing her felt like déjà vu and why he didn't mind when she called him Raphael.

Chapter Eleven

The Wiley Supermarket offices were larger than expected, Lyla thought nervously. It was her first time on the hallowed top floor of the company. She had done her interview on the third floor with a friendly HR assistant two floors down. And now she was at the top floor sitting in the waiting room with Brandi, they were pretending to read the magazines on the table.

They had arrived early to avoid the traffic and not to feel rushed. That meant the offices had not come alive yet. Slowly the staff trickled in, but they were alone in the waiting room.

"Oh my goodness, look," Brandi whistled, "to your right."

Lyla swung around and looked. Three men were talking near the bank of the elevators. They were almost on the same height; one was obviously bulkier than the other two. The hunky one laughed at something one of the men said and then he turned around and caught her looking.

She lowered her eyes quickly.

"Someone needs to tell me if this is a modeling agency or a supermarket." Brandi murmured. "Look at them. Goodness."

The one who had caught her looking headed in their direction and then stopped.

"Hello Ladies." He stopped in front of her and said pleasantly. "How may I help?"

Brandi was looking at him with her mouth half opened. It was left up to her to do the talking. Lyla was smiling nervously.

"We are interns. We are supposed to be working up here at executive offices. I am Lyla Wiley, and that is Brandi Phillips."

"Oh, you ladies are early. My name is Walter Wiley."

"That means you are the CFO!" Brandi said shaking her Wiley Bizz Magazine, "I have been reading up.".

He smiled at Brandi and then turned to Lyla. "I hope you enjoy your time here at the Wiley Group of companies, Lyla and Brandi."

The men who were talking came into the reception area, one of them had green eyes. That one was Saint. Lyla surmised the other one was Preston. She had seen him in business magazines before.

They introduced themselves.

Saint and Walter watched her to the point of her feeling like squirming. Just when she thought that she couldn't take it anymore the elevator doors opened, and another Wiley brother came through it.

This one resembled Preston, he just had curly hair like Case. She assumed he was Jordan. She was right.

"Are Case and Guy here yet?" Jordan asked impatiently before he came into the reception area fully.

"No." Walter was the one who answered.

"Good. I need to make a call." Jordan paused. "I'll take it

in Preston's office."

He paused when he saw Lyla. He looked from his brothers to her and then grinned. "I am assuming this is Lyla?"

"Yes." Lyla cleared her throat.

"Lovely to meet you." Jordan shook her hand. "How was Barbados?"

"Good." Lyla nodded. "It was good."

Case had told them about her and them going to Barbados. Why hadn't she considered that before? She was not going to be anonymous working in the building.

"I'll see you around, Lyla," Jordan said briskly.

"Sure." Lyla nodded.

He smiled and walked away.

"Conference Room Two," Preston called after him.

"Okay." Jordan gave a thumbs up. Walter and Preston left in the direction of what she assumed was Conference Room Two.

Saint stayed behind and gave her an intense stare before nodding and walking behind his brothers.

"Oh for the love of all that is holy and good and deep in this world, they can't all be related and so pretty." Brandy pretended to fan herself. "I thought Case was handsome, but these guys have variety for every taste."

The elevator opened and Brandy stopped talking. She gasped aloud.

Lyla giggled. Case had said women fainted when Guy walked down the street. She had thought he was exaggerating, but she could see what he was talking about now.

Guy was not like the others. He wasn't in a suit. He was in jeans that had a rip in it. And a light blue dress shirt that he didn't bother to tuck in. He was seriously handsome. He looked a lot like Case, a slightly shorter, slimmer version of her husband.

She closed her eyes briefly.

She needed to stop it. She was calling Case her husband in her head since she left Barbados on Friday. Since he dropped her at the airport and told her he would pop in and see her on Monday because he had a quarterly shareholder meeting at the main office. Since he had kissed her on her cheek. Since he texted her Saturday night just to tell her hi.

"Good morning," Guy said pleasantly and then paused.

"Conference Room Two," Lyla said helpfully. "I am assuming you are here for the quarterly meeting."

"Yes." Guy looked at her fully and then smiled. "Thank you er…"

"Lyla."

"Lyla," Guy smiled even wider. "Hey, nice to meet you."

He shook her hand vigorously. "This is the first day here, huh?

"Yes. Lyla nodded. "I am looking forward to it."

"All the best. You'll do great."

He headed for Conference Room Two and Brandi glared at her enviously. "You are one lucky girl."

"Shut up." Lyla grinned.

"Are any of them single?" Brandi picked up a magazine, "I am asking for a friend."

"Which friend?" Lyla chuckled.

"My imaginary friend." Brandi laughed. "So is the green-eyed one taken? Or the hunky Walter? Talk Lyla!"

"They are all married," Lyla whispered. "Tell your friend to cool it."

"I'll tell her," Brandi smirked. "That's not a Wiley brother is it?"

Brandi pointed to a cleanly shaven dark-skinned man who looked like he could rival Walter Wiley in the hunky department.

"I don't think so." Lyla murmured. "He doesn't look like them."

"But he is fine." Brandi whistled. "I am not going to get any work done here, am I?"

"You'll settle down," Lyla whispered. "Hopefully."

The man headed in their direction and greeted them.

"Good morning. I am Arthur Jones. HR Admin and the person responsible for the management trainees. Mr. Wiley said you were up here early and ready to work. He likes that. You two made quite an impression on him."

Arthur grinned. "You have one up on the other three trainees. Good job. We'll go to Conference Room One and wait for them before we get started. The receptionist will send them through. I am excited about the project this year. Can't wait to talk about it."

Lyla felt a shaft of disappointment; she was looking forward to seeing Case step out of the elevator, but she got up and followed Arthur to the conference room. The other conference room was a fully glassed and across from Conference Room One.

She would still get to see Case.

****

"Sorry I am late." Case walked into the meeting nearly fifteen minutes after the start with a cup of green tea in hand. "Somebody should have woken me up."

"I called you," Preston who was in mid-sentence paused to answer. "You said, I'll be there shortly."

"I sleep talk," Case mumbled. "Why couldn't we have this meeting at home anyway. We are the only shareholders in the Wiley Group, and most of us live at the same place."

Guy chuckled. "I said the same thing."

"We discussed this." Preston frowned. "It is easier to meet here. You two said yes to the venue."

Case made a face.

"He is such a baby." Saint chuckled. "He wants to roll out of bed and have a meeting."

"A married baby." Walter grinned, "have you seen his wife? She is going to cause trouble in the office."

"What do you mean?" Case asked sitting down.

"Look at Arthur, he is drooling and trying hard to cover it." Saint nodded to the conference room across from the one they were in. "And the two male interns look like they are competing for her attention."

Case swung around in his chair and saw Lyla; her hair tumbled around her in waves, a smile on her face as she talked animatedly to Arthur who did look a little awestruck. The other two guys had varying degrees of that look on their face too.

"You should go in there," Walter said, "greet her, say hi honey, kiss her on the forehead and walk out. That will make them back off."

"No," Preston growled, "I want a level playing field here. There is to be no special treatment of any of the interns especially, Lyla. This year we are doing something different. The interns will get a more in-depth look at all areas of the business.

"We are rolling out a new product under our newest beauty brand, Honey and Silk. The interns will be in charge of it with support from the main staff of course."

"What better way to get them acquainted with all the departments but to give them something tangible to do?" Walter grinned. "I like the idea."

"It was Arthur's idea," Preston said, "he said last year's interns complained about being bored. These will not be, not by a long shot."

Case had not dragged his eyes from Lyla. He heard his brothers talking, but for the life of him, he couldn't look away.

She was talking to the guy to her right and then she felt his eyes on her, and she looked up.

She gave him a smile and a small wave.

He did the same.

He swung around and looked at his brothers when he heard them chuckling in the background. He still had the goofy smile. He couldn't quite hide it. "So, I like her."

"And what about Fifi?" Saint asked.

"She broke up with me." Case frowned. "You can forget about investigating her. We are not going to tie the knot."

"Sure," Saint murmured. "I am happy not to waste resources on Fifi Daniels. I found out something about her though. She changed her name."

"Maybe that's because she was adopted," Case murmured. "She escaped the same fate as Lyla."

"If you were going to marry her, I would find out her name," Saint shrugged, "but since you are not. It's over for me."

"So what are you going to do about your current wife?" Jordan asked lazily.

"I don't know." Case was itching to look back at Lyla again.

"I think we all know he wants to keep her." Walter chuckled. "Look at his face; he's pretending that he doesn't want to pursue her. Pathetic. You know what this reminds me of? The cat and mouse games Jordan and Shawn played for years."

"Leave me out of this," Jordan muttered, he was lazily swinging in his chair. "It's more like a Guy and Lucia situation. He was her benefactor for years, remember?"

"But Lucia didn't know I was her benefactor," Guy said. "She liked me because of me. She thought I was poor. She ditched a rich doctor who could offer her the world for little old me. Case, on the other hand, is rich, good looking, a popular singer. He bailed her out of a bad situation, the Wiley name is a well-known one. You are all she has. Case doesn't have to lift a finger to win her over. She would probably do anything for him; she is his modern mail-order bride."

Case glared at Guy. "Why are you so cruel?"

"Just telling the truth." Guy shrugged. "You are all she has. She is obligated to love you."

"She has parents." Case growled.

"Really?" Guy smirked, "you mean like the mother that sold her? And who knows who her father is."

"Her father is unknown, according to her birth certificate, but if you want me to dig deeper I can," Saint offered.

Case shook his head. "I have a suspicion who her father is. In that regard Barbados was useful."

"What's the suspicion?" Saint, Walter, and Jordan almost asked in unison.

Case chuckled. "I think that Jules may be her father."

"Julius Harvey?" Preston frowned. "How?"

"He was in Cuba at the time of her conception. She resembles his mother Sienna, and he knew this Maria girl who was an exotic dancer that he had a one-night stand with who cooked him vaca frita. He keeps harping on about it."

"But I thought her biological's mother's name was Valentina Martinez?" Saint asked. "How could it be Maria?"

"Maybe Maria was her stage name." Case shrugged. "Here's another twist. Apparently, the exotic dancer, Maria, looks like Fifi. That's all Jules talks about these days."

"Your ex-fiancée, Fifi Daniels?" Jordan asked incredulously.

"One and the same." Case murmured.

"Lyla just became interesting again." Saint drummed his fingers on the table. "I love mysteries."

"Unfortunately, I might not be able to get to the bottom of all of this in the next couple of weeks. Sandy is on the verge of giving birth, it might be this week, it might be next week, and I have a million and one business related things to do."

"When can we move on with our company business?" Preston asked impatiently as if he was not as intrigued as they were by the situation.

"Now." Case nodded. He swung around to see Lyla again, but she and the rest of the group had left the conference room.

****

"You know which actress you look like?" Arthur sat across from Lyla; they were at lunch in the executive dining room. The executive dining room had their own chef and wait staff, and the menu was varied, they could have things as simple as sandwiches or as complex as galantine.

"Try the galantine." Arthur had whispered to them as soon as they stepped into the dining room.

Arthur had strategically placed the interns to have lunch with various executives, to schmooze as he called it. She had gotten the coveted pairing with Preston Wiley.

However, he was running late, and Arthur was making conversation with her as they both ate the delicious galantine with roasted vegetables.

Lyla had never had vegetables that tasted so good. She almost forgot to answer Arthur as she tucked into her meal.

"Aren't you going to guess?" Arthur asked raising an eyebrow.

"Zoe Saldana." Lyla smiled the actress. "Brandi tells me

that all the time."

"She is right." Arthur nodded.

"I don't see it." Lyla played with her salad.

"I knew you'd say that people usually don't see it." Arthur chuckled. "So how are you liking your day at the Wiley Group?"

"I love it." Lyla didn't want to appear as if she was gushing, but she truly liked the work environment. They were working on a real project with real-life consequences. All five of them even had their own desks with their names on it. The business took its trainees seriously.

"Today and the rest of the week is the honeymoon period." Arthur smiled, "after that, you all are going to be treated like regular staff."

"Got it." Lyla nodded.

"If you have any queries or concerns, I am your man," Arthur added.

"Thank you," Lyla smiled back.

"I should allow you to get settled in first but…" Arthur quirked a brow, his brown eyes softened. "Let's just put it out there, you are pretty, and I like you and would like to get to know you better."

"I ah…" Lyla opened her mouth, "I ah…"

"No need to feel pressured. Arthur grinned. "I am not your immediate supervisor, just the orientation man. I can't fire you. I have no undue influence where you are concerned. You can say no to going out with me, and it will not affect your job. My ego, on the other hand, will take a beating but I recover quickly. No worries."

Lyla smiled. "You are covering all the bases with that addendum, Arthur."

"I work in HR." Arthur chuckled. "I do not want you to feel harassed or pressured in any way. This company takes that kind of thing very seriously.

"Ah, here comes the boss, we'll take this conversation up later."

He got up when Preston came near and took his food to another section of the room.

Preston sat down. "Sorry, I am late, I had a conference call with the prime minister. He was trying to convince me to take up a Senate position."

One of the servers came over and took his lunch order, and Lyla stared at him wide-eyed. "Wow, what did you say?"

"Told him I'd pray about it. Serving my country would be an honor but I am not sure I have the time for it now, and I am not sure what God wants me to do. I seek him first."

"That's quite unique in business." Lyla observed. "The God-factor is slowly dying."

"For me, it's a habit," Preston shrugged. "God is the chief executive officer in my life. I am only as successful as he wants me to be."

"And that's your secret to success," Lyla asked, "putting God first?"

"Pretty much," Preston nodded. "That and hard work. In the early days, I worked myself into the ground. My brother Jordan and I were just eighteen when we took over the reins of the Wiley Supermarket."

"And you still managed to raise your family and make it a success." Lyla added. "I read an article about you. It's a remarkable story."

"I had help." Preston's food was served, and he tucked in. "I mostly raised my youngest brother though. He feels more like a son than a brother."

"Case." Lyla linked her fingers together. Suddenly she was nervous; she expected a rebuke, a warning for her to stay away from Case because she was a gold digger who entrapped him into marrying her. Wasn't that how they did it in the movies? The family members gave the outsiders warnings.

Preston looked at her suddenly guarded expression and seemed to read her mind. "I am not going to interfere in Case's life. He is an adult he makes his own decisions. We raised him to be smart and caring and helpful.

"I am more interested in you right now, your professional growth because you are my management trainee. However, your scenario with Case plays out, you should take advantage of the opportunity to be a trainee here. Strive to be the best and who knows when you graduate next year, you'll have a job here."

Lyla relaxed slightly. "I will. Thank you, Mr. Wiley."

"Preston." He smiled. "We practice a first name basis culture at the Wiley Group of companies."

Lyla nodded. "I realized that I thought that you would be different because you are the head of the place."

"Not really the head." Preston smiled, "I have to report to the shareholders. I serve at their discretion."

Arthur passed by the table before Lyla could reply and winked at her. "Conference room two at 1:30."

"I'll be there." Lyla nodded and then looked at Preston's knowing expression.

"Don't let Arthur or any of the others distract you," Preston warned. "They'll be yapping at your heels like a band of hyenas, keep your focus."

Lyla grinned. "I can handle myself. I am accustomed to it from school."

Preston smiled. "Well then, I look forward to seeing you shine, Lyla."

He looked near the door and waved.

Lyla sat up straighter in her seat and looked behind her. It was Case.

He came over, smiling. "I heard that it was lunch time."

He sat across from her and beside Preston. "Hey, Lyla Wiley."

"Hi." Lyla smiled.

"Has my brother finished telling you that you should stay focused and not let me be a distraction?"

Lyla chuckled. "Something like that."

"You are so predictable." Case elbowed Preston.

Preston gave him a mock frown. "Don't you have things to do?"

"Yes, as a matter of fact, I do. I just came to deliver a message to Lyla. My sister-in-law Sheryl is cordially inviting you to dinner with her family Friday evening."

"Isn't that your family, Preston? Lyla asked. I met Sheryl in the sales department today. She was nice."

"Yes." Preston nodded.

"I'd love to come." Lyla touched Case's hand briefly.

He looked down at where their hands touched and then cleared his throat. "So Lyla how is it going?"

"Good." Lyla smiled.

"I read that book about Love Languages that you insisted I read." Case raised an eyebrow. "It was interesting. I think my love language is quality time."

"He got up. I'll be at the studio. The modern looking building across from this one. I'll be there until six. You can stop by if you want and speak my love language and then you can tell me yours."

He gave her a little salute and walked away.

Chapter Twelve

Lyla was packing up her desk to visit Case after work. He had given her a broad, not so subtle hint, to come and visit him. It was all she thought about for the rest of the work day when they were briefed on their project. She had been itching for five o'clock to come. The hands on the clock moved so slowly.

"So how was your meeting with Preston?" Arthur appeared out of nowhere. She had assumed that he had already left for the day.

"It was good." Lyla rummaged in her bag for her lip gloss; she needed to freshen up her appearance before she went next door.

"Have you thought about hanging out after work?" Arthur was looking over into her bag with too much interest. She closed it and sighed.

"Arthur, I don't want to mix business with... er... dating."

"I understand," Arthur, nodded good-naturedly, "I expected

that response after I saw you with Case at lunch today. You two have something going on?"

Lyla paused before she answered. Did they have something going on? Well, she wanted to have something going. She had no idea how Case really felt. He was hard to read.

"I don't know." She answered honestly.

"Why do you have the same last name?" Arthur asked curiously. "At first, I thought you were a family member, but you don't act like it."

"How would a Wiley family member act?" Lyla asked trying to use classic misdirection and not answer. She was surprised that nobody else had remarked on it today.

"Entitled, I guess." Arthur grinned. "I don't know. That's probably how I would act if my family owned the business where I am forced to be an intern like everybody else."

"None of the Wiley's act entitled," Lyla murmured.

"So are you a niece or a cousin or something?" Arthur asked. "The Wiley's have some pretty attractive nieces? I think they are triplets. They look like models. I think one of them is a model. They stop by here sometimes."

"No." Lyla shook her head. "Not a niece. At least I don't think so. I don't know who my father is." Which was true, but it vaguely implied that she had no idea how she came up with the Wiley surname.

"Ah," Arthur nodded. "No family history, huh."

"None," Lyla replied honestly. "And just the very utterance of that made her sad. She suddenly thought of Consuela and her offhand approach to motherhood and her father who Consuela had repeatedly referred to as a deadbeat tourist."

"You should do a DNA test," Arthur suggested. "I did mine a couple of months ago, and I found a lot of relatives that way. I found out that my great grandfather was originally from Ghana and my great grandmother was from Morocco. I even found aunts and uncles and too many cousins to count."

"Wow, that's fascinating, Arthur."

"I have relatives all over the world." Arthur chuckled. "I thought it was just me and my mom and my sister here in Jamaica, but obviously I was wrong. I didn't know my father. He died before I was born. He and my mom were not in a relationship either; she didn't know much about him. Now I have a whole host of family members who want to meet me who have stories to tell me about my dad, who sent me pictures. Now I know that I resemble him greatly and that we have some of the same mannerisms. It was cool to find out. I have medical history and grandparents. It really put the puzzle together for me."

"And you think that it could happen for me too?" Lyla asked doubtfully. "Suppose no one else in my family has done a DNA test?"

"It can't hurt to try," Arthur reassured her.

"Okay." Lyla nodded. "Thank you, Arthur."

"Well uh, have a good evening." Arthur stepped back, "if you want to hear more about what I did, I'll tell you."

"Thanks." She headed to the elevator contemplatively, forgetting that she wanted to freshen up for Case. It was while she was in the middle of the parking lot that she remembered and it would be foolish to turn back now.

She passed Adam's car in the parking lot, and she waved to him. He was there to pick up Brandi so that they could spend their quality time.

Brandi had proven popular today with the people in finance and stopped by to celebrate some birthday party with her new friends.

It was a gift she coveted, the ease with which Brandi made friends.

She walked to the studio which was across the vast parking

lot and wished that she had changed her shoes.

Case was waiting for her in the spacious lobby area. It was decorated in monochrome, white, black and grey. The only splash of color was a red musical note that dominated one wall and looked as if it was vibrating.

"Hey Lyla," he smiled when she walked through the door. "Do you want a tour, or have you had it with offices for today?"

"I'd love a tour," Lyla said looking around. "The décor in here is certainly interesting.

"My sister-in-law, Shawn did it. I told her what I liked, and she ran with it."

Case pointed to a picture of him and a lady in the foyer. "That's her."

"She's Jordan's wife?" Lyla moved closer to the picture. "She is pretty."

"She is his wife, best friend, business partner, ride or die." Case mused. "They've been friends since birth."

"Relationship goals." Lyla whistled.

"Yeah," Case cleared his throat. "So, Wiley studios occupies the ground floor of the building."

"What's at the top?" Lyla asked, moving from picture to picture of various artists on the wall. She recognized quite a few of the artists.

"The first floor is rented to an animation studio and an advertising agency rents the second floor. They do a lot of business with us."

"Cool." Lyla nodded. "That's a good fit, the animation, the advertising, and the music."

"I think so too." Case grinned. "That's what I did in university actually. I did Marketing with an emphasis on advertising. I did it online. Preston and Jordan insisted. I argued with them about it, but Preston found a couple of schools that catered to non-traditional students, so I chose marketing. I liked it so much I even did the MBA."

"You have an MBA?" Lyla gasped, "I didn't know you had a degree, much less two."

"A brain is a terrible thing to waste," Case said philosophically, "and when you are idle, you get distracted. The music business gives me a lot of downtime. I used my downtime wisely. I do some production for other people. I even produce some ads for the other Wiley businesses."

"So on to our tour," Case smiled. Lyla was looking at him as if she didn't know him. Which was understandable. She didn't and he had a desire to rectify that. He wanted them to be friends.

"To the left of you is the area leading to the restrooms, and through here," he opened a door, "is the kitchenette."

"That door right across from us is the live room. That's where the vocalists sing, and instrumentalists play their instruments."

He opened the door.

"This is a specialized acoustic door. Normally, you can't hear a thing through it if someone has a session in here. The entire place is clad with acoustic panels. Once I close this door, no noise escapes this place."

"Cool." Lyla walked into the live room; it was huge. There were drums, guitars, violins, a baby grand piano and other equipment she didn't recognize. There was even a sitting area with couches strewn around.

When they entered the recessed lighting came on. Case turned on the round colorful lantern lights, and they brightened up the place even more. They were a pretty addition to the space.

"Now, this is romantic." Lyla looked around.

Case laughed. "I never thought about it like that before."

"So what happens in here?" Lyla looked around.

"This is where the instrumentalists, play and the recording engineer, the producer, and the mixing engineer, work their magic to turn the music into the sounds you hear."

Case pushed his hand in his pocket. "When I am doing an album, I spend a lot of time in here with the band."

"So this is where the magic happens," Lyla looked around, "where a Case Wiley classic is born."

"More or less." Case smiled. "Let's go. I have more to show you."

They walked out of the live room, and around a corner. There was a sign that said Offices above the door. He pushed the door, and they entered a corridor.

"That's Cleon's office. He is the studio manager. Jules' office, he is a producer and my manager, he also manages other clients too."

"My office," Case said pointing at a closed door.

He opened the door, and there was a basic desk inside, a keyboard and a chair were facing the desk.

"Spartan," Lyla chuckled.

"It looks like a junkyard when I am in here for any length of time, and I am right beside Jean. Who is our heavenly overworked admin assistant and her assistants?"

Jean's office was opened. There were three desks in there.

She was on the phone, she waved to Lyla and covered the mouthpiece. "You are gorgeous. Who is she, Case? Are we still doing the ads for the pageant?"

"I don't know." Case grinned. "This is Lyla, my friend."

Lyla waved when Jean got back on the phone.

"Through here is the main office." She saw several desks with computer monitors and various sound equipment. Two men were standing beside Jules who was pointing to something on the screen before him. They looked up and waved when she and Case walked in.

"They are finalizing the video I did in Barbados," Case said. "You'll meet them at another time. Through here is the control room. Now, this is where you get your vocals done."

There were various glass enclosed areas with microphones in the ceiling. It was huge.

"Now in here, it is all about your voice." Case sat in front of one of the glassed off areas in front of a bank of equipment. If you want, you can go through the glassed area madam and sing in the central microphone," Case said in a flourish. "I will record a track for you. Play it back so that you can hear yourself."

Lyla did as she was told. "You could have a choir in here."

"I think there was a choir here earlier. The studio is usually fully booked." Case steepled his finger under his chin. "Can you hear me?"

"Yes." Lyla gave him a thumbs up.

"Want to try a song?"

"Sure." Lyla grinned.

"What's your favorite?"

"Gospel or secular?

"Anyone that comes to mind," Case said.

"Killing me softly, the Roberta Flack version," Lyla said sheepishly. "She always heard the song and thought of him."

"Interesting choice," Case murmured. "Do you like a particular singer?"

"Yes." Lyla nodded eagerly.

Case grinned. "Well take a shot at it."

"I heard he sang a good song, I heard he had a style, And so I came to see him, to listen for a while, And there he was, this young boy, a stranger to my eyes…

Lyla started off tentatively and then realized that the background music for the song played. And then she really got into it.

She closed her eyes and belted out the lyrics. She didn't see Case's expression or that Jules had entered the control room. His mouth was hanging open when she opened her eyes.

Case was blinking rapidly. His voice was husky when she finished. "Thank you, Lyla. You have a beautiful voice."

"Is she signed to anybody?" Jules asked Case.

"No," Case whispered. "I was not hallucinating just now was I?"

"I heard it," Jules said, drawing up a chair and sitting beside Case. "Play it back."

Lyla came out of the sound booth and grinned. "Hey, that's me."

"And you sound great!" Jules said excitedly. "Can you come and do a demo for me tomorrow?"

Lyla looked between him and Case. "Okay."

"You sound more than great." Case shook his head. "I am actually stunned."

"Stunned," Jules repeated. "I have some songs I was going to give to a client of mine, but your voice is better suited for them."

"What?" Lyla sank down into the chair nearest her and looked in Jules' excited eyes confusedly. "I sounded that good."

"Yes," Jules nodded, "come and do a demo tomorrow and I'll know for sure."

"I have work." Lyla muttered, "I am a management trainee."

"I know. Come in the evening." Jules stood up, "I knew getting you out of Cuba was the best thing we had ever done."

He exited the room, grinning from ear to ear.

Lyla looked at Case, "now is the time to tell me that I stank and that Jules has a hearing problem. Don't worry I won't mind."

"It's the opposite actually." Case shook his head. "You sound good. You handled that song like a pro."

"Why, thank you." Lyla laughed, "my favorite singers are C. Wiley and Roberta Flack. I know all their lyrics by heart."

"Beautiful voice from a beautiful lady," Case said contemplatively. "You want us to go get something to eat?"

"Sure." Lyla nodded. "Maybe then we can surprise each other some more. You with your MBA, me with my singing."

Case nodded. "Yes, let's go."

Chapter Thirteen

"**I** hardly see you anymore," Brandi whined as Lyla got ready to meet Case for her date at Preston Wiley's house.

"That's because you are busy being Miss Popular." Lyla tried on a brighter lipstick than usual and then rubbed it off. It was a family dinner, not technically a date. Just like all her time spent with Case this week. They hung out at lunch, most days at the studio and then they hung out after work. Brandi was right, they hardly saw each other anymore, and it was mostly because she was busy with Case.

"So where are you going?" Brandi stood at the door in her oversized t-shirt with a bowl of cereal in hand.

"I was invited to a family dinner." Lyla looked at Brandi sideways. "Preston Wiley's house."

Brandi whistled. "Are you serious?"

"Yes, his wife invited me."

"I hear that they have a son that's close to our age. He is eighteen, I think. Find out if he is single."

"No." Lyla shook her head.

"Oh come on," Brandi batted her eyelashes, "I am asking for a friend."

"The same imaginary friend?" Lyla chuckled.

"Yes, her, and Misty from work too. She says she knows them because they go to the same church. She says that Pete, that is the name of the son, looks just like his dad. He is a young version of Preston Wiley. Take a selfie with him."

"No." Lyla grimaced.

"Spoilsport." Brandi shook her head at Lyla. "Lucky for you, I am going to spend the weekend at Adam's. His mom and dad are celebrating thirty years together. I'll be there all weekend; they packed it with activities and parties. I'll see you at work Monday. I am leaving from there to work. I hear there is a beach trip to Negril on Sunday. I am for it. I'll tell Jerry you said hi."

"Okay, have fun." Lyla smiled. "And do not say hi to Jerry from me. Do not encourage him."

"Ha." Brandi finished her cereal and then gave her a thumbs up, "You have fun too. By the way, love that dress. It fits your shape to the t. You will wow the family."

"Thanks." Lyla looked at the dress in the mirror; it was a red and black swirl piece. She knew Case's favorite color was red and she had dished it out of the closet. She had liked the A-line cut and the cap sleeves and the feel of the material, and now she had Brandi's approval. She hoped she wowed the family as she had said, but she would settle for them just being friendly.

She was nervous about this. She had moved from never having seeing Case for years to suddenly seeing him every day. She no longer had a crush on him. She had gone way past that. He was entertaining and funny, and he got her. She didn't think it was an act either. Case was a genuine sort of person and he excited her. She couldn't think of a time in her life when she was this energized to get up in the mornings and looked forward to the day ahead. Most of that had to do with Case.

Her phone started buzzing. She had forgotten to put on the ringer. She picked it up; it was Case.

"Hey, I am at your gate," Case said. "Can you tell your security to let me in."

"Sure." Lyla smiled. Technically this was his apartment, which meant it was his security. She was living on Case's largesse.

It wasn't something that he would appreciate hearing though. She knew that much about him; Case was not particularly comfortable with effusive gratitude. One thanks was enough for him. Constantly telling him thanks annoyed him. She took one last look at herself. Her skin was glowing, this past week her few stray zits had disappeared entirely. She inhaled, called the security, and made sure her living room was neat.

She told Brandi bye and left the apartment.

Case's car was a late model Audi Q5. The interior had a new, clean smell. He had the radio on. She recognized the voice of Bill Withers. Case had gallantly opened her passenger door and then slipped back into the car.

"I like this car," Lyla looked around. "This is my first time in a new car."

Case nodded solemnly, "I like it too."

"And it's red." Lyla chuckled.

Case smiled. He was dressed in black from head to toe—a casual polo shirt and black pants. He was wearing a neat gold watch. He looked very urbane and sophisticated. Lyla couldn't believe that she was here now with him like this.

She turned to the road and dragged her eyes from his. Bill

Withers' song, Ain't No Sunshine, came on.

"I love this song. This was Sienna's favorite artiste. He is the one that sings Lovely Day and Just The Two of Us."

"Yes! And more. He is one of my favorites too, love his lyrics." Case chuckled. "I was thinking of covering one of his songs, Lean on Me, for a personal project, A Case of Love. It's about my life and the songs that speak to it. Most of them would be covers. I am working on a couple of original pieces though."

"That sounds great." Lyla turned to him. "I can't wait to hear it."

"Maybe we can do a duet." Case smiled. "We'll see."

Lyla grinned. "Yes!"

"I don't know when," Case murmured. "Jules thinks that I should stick to the brand. So I do the gospel album. We have the songs already. I'll be in studio for close to a month, and then we'll work on the project."

"That's great." Lyla smiled. "Perfect. That means you'll be here."

"I'll be here for the entire summer except for a week in Canada." Case drove out of the complex. "Did I tell you, you are looking lovely this evening."

Lyla chuckled, "I was just thinking the same thing about you."

Case reached for her hand and squeezed it. She squeezed it back.

It was only when they reached the stoplight. That he released her hand, that coincided with the song Lean on Me.

They started singing the song together, Sometimes in our lives we all have pain, We all have sorrow, But if we are wise, We know that there's always tomorrow...

Their voices blended so well that when they reached the bridge of the song, if you need a friend, call me...Case slowed the car to almost a crawl. They finished the song together.

And Case laughed. "I can't believe this. We make perfect harmony."

"We do." Lyla beamed, "we really do."

"And I meant every word," Case said seriously, starting the car again. "If there is one song that can describe the relationship with my brothers this is it. I am now extending it to you. Welcome to the brotherhood."

Lyla laughed. "Thank you."

****

The brothers lived in a townhouse complex together — all of them. Lyla was trying to wrap her mind around the fact that when they drove through the iron gates, she was not driving into some expensive hotel. The landscaping was outstanding, and the layout was pretty.

To the left of them were three townhouses, Jordan, Walter, and Guy, to the right was Preston, Saint, and Case.

Case stopped in front of his place. "I can give you a tour after." He smiled at her. "And you can meet Ferb and Phineas."

"I feel special." Lyla batted her eyelash at him, "I am getting to meet your cats."

"As you should," Case said, "I don't introduce just anyone to Ferb and Phin."

"Did Fifi meet them?" Lyla wondered out loud.

"No." Case grinned at her, "you look pretty when you are jealous."

"I am not jealous," Lyla said unconvincingly.

They passed the townhouse beside Case's. There were a

few cars parked in the driveway.

"Saint has people over," Case said, "maybe Sandy's folks. They are frequent visitors; she is almost ready to give birth to twins."

"Does she have twins in her family?"

"Yes," Case nodded. "She has an identical twin sister who tried to fool everyone into thinking she was Sandrene. That was nearly a year ago. They were so identical it was hard for everyone to tell them apart. Everyone but Saint. He knows his girl."

"Wow," Lyla whispered. "You are surrounded by romance."

"And yet, none rubbed off on me." Case shook his head in mock despair.

Lyla was still chuckling when Case pressed the buzzer for Preston's house. She paused when she saw the bonsai trees at the front.

"Oh my goodness, that's a mango tree, she went closer to the plant. It has on fruit."

She looked up when the door opened, and a younger replica of Preston appeared in the doorway.

She straightened up, forgetting the mango plant. It was true, the son and the father were one. She was sure that there was a religious lesson in there.

"Hey Case," Pete greeted Case and bumped his fist. "And Lyla?"

Lyla came closer and nodded. "Has anybody ever told you, you are a younger version of Preston?"

"Everyone." Pete grinned. "The older I get, the more I hear it. Come on in. Be relaxed. It's family night tonight. Both my parents are usually mellow at this time."

And they were. It was strange to see Preston in a family setting. He was in a blue polo shirt and jeans; his daughter was in his arms, she squealed when she saw Case.

"Cake!" She called out. "It's uncle Cake!"

"Will somebody correct this child as to my right name?" Case said taking her from her father and receiving a loud smack on both cheeks from the pretty little girl.

Case held her close. "How is my gorgeous, intelligent, sweetie pie?"

"She's a brat." Preston answered, "tell your uncle how much of a brat you are."

"I am not a brat." Petra declared. She peered around Case's shoulder and looked at Lyla shyly. She was a beautiful combination of both parents. She had Preston's complexion and eyes and her mother's cute button nose and lips. She was truly a little beauty.

"Hello, Lyla." Preston nodded to her.

"Welcome Lyla," Sheryl said warmly. She was dressed in a loosely flowing maxi dress which highlighted her toned arms.

She did not look like she could be a mother to Pete. Lyla thought, she looked like a big sister.

She said as much.

Sheryl laughed. "Thank you."

"I get it all the time." Pete grinned. "When I go out with her, I have to scare off men who are checking out my mom."

"Case introduce Petra to Lyla, will you?" Preston said. "She is looking over your shoulder and waiting for it."

Case turned to Lyla. "Lyla this little lady is my niece, Petra Wiley. Petra this is my, er, friend, Lyla."

"Hello, Petra." Lyla waved.

The little girl waved back, her eyes wide. "I like her, Uncle Cake."

"I do too." Case grinned over at Lyla. "You got the Petra approval."

"And that's a big deal." Sheryl laughed, "Queen Petra

dishes out favors sparingly."

"Come let's sit and get to know one another better." Sheryl smiled. "Dinner will be served shortly. I am just reheating Blossom's lasagna. I hope you like lasagna, Lyla."

"I do." Lyla nodded.

They sat in the living room which was cheery and modern. Sheryl cuddled up to Preston who casually had his hand around her shoulders.

Lyla looked at them enviously. It was obvious that they were in love.

Pete sat on the edge of the chair beside them. Case sat beside her in the single chair. Petra was sitting on his lap.

They looked like a picture-perfect family. And they were warm and inclusive. They got along well together bantering back and forth, including her in their exchange.

Sheryl was a master in making her feel relaxed. It was like seeing a master at work. They talked about themselves and their family.

Preston mentioned that Walter was insisting on throwing a party for Jordan in July. "I escaped him this year because I was out of town."

"I didn't escape him, Case grinned. He took a cake to the studio and had everybody sing me happy birthday."

"He has an events calendar." Pete chuckled. "All of our birthdays are on it. I think Uncle Jordan's birthday will be a cluster party where he will celebrate more than one thing."

"Ah," Preston frowned. "That's why he was so excited."

"Yep." Pete chuckled. "And expect some gender reveal parties soon, Aunty Aisha and Shawn were talking about it. They both want to have boys, and they are both planning to give their sons the middle name Joseph.

"Aunty Shawn said her son would be Cairo Joseph Wiley and Aunty Aisha would name hers William Joseph Wiley."

"You need to stop gossiping with your aunts." Preston chuckled.

"It can't be helped." Pete shook his head. "The baby fever is real in this complex, and they were over here for lunch. Miss Blossom's strawberry cheesecake is a hit."

"Do you want children, Lyla?" Sheryl asked a calculating gleam in her eye.

"Yes." Lyla nodded vigorously. "I love them. I wouldn't mind having a couple."

"A couple?" Preston raised an eyebrow and then smiled. "Why not?"

"Case loves children too." Sheryl inserted smoothly. "Just look at him and Petra."

Pete laughed. "I think girls on a whole love Case, from tiny ones to grannies."

Case didn't rise to the bait. He looked at Lyla and gave her a half smile.

Lyla wished she knew what he was thinking, but he changed the subject smoothly. "Maybe you should tell Walter that Lyla's birthday is the same as Jordan's."

"Really?" Preston asked, "July the fifth?"

"Yes." Lyla nodded "I had no idea that we shared the same birthday."

"I hear that you sing, Lyla. You should do a duet with Case." Pete changed the subject from birthdays.

Lyla nodded. "I might if asked nicely."

"I'll ask nicely." Case grinned. Petra chose that moment to leave his lap and headed for her father's.

"I sing too," Pete said, "not so much these days though. I spend a lot of my time working."

"He designs and sells game apps." Case explained to Lyla. "He is a little multi-millionaire."

"Ah, stop it." Pete fanned off his uncle with a grin.

"A multi-millionaire who doesn't want to go to college." Preston sighed. "Tell him Case that you did it even though you didn't want to."

"I did it," Case said to Pete. "It's a Wiley tradition."

"It is," Preston said, "that and the fact that I am concerned about your social life. It is not healthy to sit around your computer and not talk to real people."

"I talk to Giselle," Pete said grinning. "Remember her?"

"My cousin Giselle?" Case asked raising his eyebrows.

"Yes." Pete nodded. "That's right; she is your cousin, not mine. Right, Dad? Giselle and I are in no way related."

Preston sighed loudly. "No, you are not."

"And she is just three years older than I am," Pete continued. "That's not old is it?"

"Can we change the subject?" Sheryl asked quickly, "we have a guest. We can talk about other things but Giselle."

Pete looked at Lyla apologetically. "Sorry, Giselle is a hot button topic around here. They get agitated whenever her name comes up. Apparently, she's an older woman who is about to ruin me."

Preston whispered something in Sheryl's ear, and they both looked resigned.

The doorbell rang. And Pete got up. "That's probably her."

"You should have said that Giselle was stopping by," Sheryl said breezily, but her facial expression was anything but relaxed.

"I never usually do." Pete shrugged. "She just shows up."

"When did this start?" Case asked curiously.

"Two years ago," Preston muttered. "He was helping her to fix her computer or something. You know she did Biology, right? She wants to become a doctor. She is finishing this year with the highest grades at her university."

Case nodded. "That's great."

"What's not great is how inseparable they are. It worries me and Sheryl. Pete is too intense about her."

Case smiled. "He is your son. Maybe that's where he got the intensity from."

Preston made a face. "That's what worries me."

And then Giselle entered the room after a whispered conversation with Pete in the foyer.

Lyla who had been sitting back in the chair watching the dynamics with the family was quite pleased to see that they were not a cookie cutter happy family. They had issues just like everybody else.

Personally, she thought that Preston was needlessly worrying about Pete. He seemed to be quite mature.

She was silently thinking these things when Giselle walked into the room, and she stifled a gasp. The girl was pretty. Exotic looking with her fine features, creamy peanut butter complexion, and thickly lashed eyes. She had curly thick midnight black hair that tumbled almost to her hips when she moved.

Lyla wondered enviously if her hair was real and tried to stifle the urge to touch her thinner, finer strands.

Giselle wore a blue tracksuit and basic white trainers. She was lithe and shapely, and Pete was obviously smitten with her.

"Hello everybody," she said politely and then she spotted Case.

"Case!" She went over to Case and hugged him.

"Hey Gis!" Case hugged her back.

"How've you been?" Giselle asked, "between track practice, bio studies and your touring, we are losing touch. Barely get a token hello on WhatsApp. I listen to your song God and Life when I train though."

Case grinned. "Thanks for the support, little cousin. Meet

Lyla."

Lyla smiled. "Hello."

"Hey," Giselle looked at her curiously. "So you are 'the' Lyla, I have been keeping up with family news. You are Case's bride from Cuba?"

Lyla cleared her throat and glanced at Case. "Well technically…"

"Typical Case, taking things slow. You'll have a lot of ice to break to get into his heart. I hope you have an ice pick." Giselle grinned. "But he is worth the effort. I can vouch for him. He is a good catch."

"My goodness," Case muttered. "She is just a friend."

"Your wife should always be your friend." Giselle smiled at Lyla. "Right, Case?"

"Okay, let's eat," Preston said, breaking up the conversation and rescuing Case from a comeback. "I am assuming you are staying for dinner, Giselle?"

"Yes, why not?" Giselle glanced at Pete. "Is that okay with you?"

"Sure." Pete nodded.

Something was wrong between them. Lyla could pick that up. Preston and Sheryl did too, they looked at each other and raised their eyebrows.

She wished though that Case had gotten a chance to respond.

Chapter Fourteen

"It was a good dinner," Lyla said after they left Preston's house. "You have a normal family. I love the dynamic with Sheryl and Preston and Pete, even Petra and her little outbursts. I envy that."

Case nodded. "What do you think about Giselle and Pete?"

"They seem fine, well something is a little off." Lyla shrugged. "Maybe they had a tiff. Friends have those sometimes."

"Giselle and Pete are obviously an item." Case shook his head in disbelief. "I can't believe it. It feels weird to me."

"Why?" Lyla looked at him in the glare of the lights in front of his house.

"I don't know." Case ran his fingers through his hair. "She is Giselle, my cousin who looks a lot like my mom and he is Pete, my nephew who looks a lot like my dad. It's weird. Like a younger version of my parents hooking up."

Lyla leaned on the car and Case rotated his neck in circles.

"You are taking this badly."

"Maybe, not really." Case sighed. "None of this is my business. I don't even know if there is anything significant between them."

"Oh there is something, at least on Pete's side," Lyla covered a yawn. "He looks at her with a kind of helpless intensity. His parents hate it. I could see Sheryl gritting her teeth in impotence, and Preston looked like he wanted to send Pete to his room and lock him up until he is thirty."

Case chuckled. "I didn't see that."

"I am observant like that," Lyla said sleepily. "But then again even Stevie Wonder could see that Pete has a giant crush.

"A crush?" Case murmured. "What does that feel like?"

"You have never had a crush?" Lyla widened her eyes. "Never in all your twenty-six years?"

"No." Case chuckled.

"But what about Fifi, you were engaged to her," Lyla asked incredulously.

"I liked her. I liked talking to her. We spent most of our two years in a long-distance relationship. Have you ever had a crush?"

"Yes." Lyla nodded. "Oh yes."

"Describe it." Case smiled at her slowly. She could see his teeth flash in the half dark and for a minute she wondered if she was ever going to get used to his smile.

"Well... er…" Lyla cleared her throat, "a crush is a desire to see and spend time with a person you find captivating. It doesn't have to be looks. It could be intellectual. It's like an intense admiration. They capture your imagination. You think of them more than you think of yourself. You wonder how it would be if you are romantically involved with them. Sometimes you fantasize about it, and it becomes all that you think about."

"Like a fixation?" Case asked.

"Well, I guess, sometimes the fixation is short lived," Lyla murmured. "Sometimes, the crush does not last long especially if you get to know the person and the fantasy and the reality are not the same. Sometimes it fades on its own."

"So have you ever acted on a crush?" Case asked folding his arms.

"I er…" Lyla cleared her throat, thinking about him. "I er…got the opportunity to meet a crush."

"And what happened?" Case asked huskily.

"The reality was better than the fantasy." Lyla looked away from him. "It's not a crush anymore."

"What is it?" Case asked.

"I'd rather not say," Lyla murmured.

Case didn't say anything after that. They stood and watched the surprisingly busy complex.

Saint and Sandrene came out and told their guests goodbye. Pete and Giselle were arguing by her car.

Saint waved to them.

They waved back.

"She is very pregnant," Lyla said in the silence referring to Sandrene who looked as if she was waddling.

Lyla yawned so loudly her jaw made a cracking sound.

"I guess a house tour now would be pointless?" Case said. "You seem bushed."

"I am. Can I take a raincheck on the tour?" Lyla murmured. "I think I have just enough energy to walk into my apartment."

Case turned to her and tucked a stray hair behind her ear. "Well, let's go then."

"They didn't speak on the way back." Case stopped in front of the townhouse. "You are number four or six?"

"Four," Lyla smiled. "Haven't you checked it out before?

After all, you pay the rent."

Case looked at her and shook his head. "No, there is no rent. I bought it for you. I guess Rita never told you?"

"No." Lyla shook her head.

"Well, it was supposed to be your new start place, when we annulled the marriage."

"Oh," Lyla frowned. "I see."

"There goes your disapproving, 'I see'." Case chuckled. "I did not know you then; an annulment was very much on the table."

"And now?" Lyla turned to him.

"Now?" Case inhaled raggedly. "Now, I am not sure."

Lyla straightened up, "Would you like to see the place?"

"Not if you want to sleep." Case turned to her.

"Well, I am awake now." Lyla blinked rapidly.

"Let's go." It was a few short steps to the front door. The townhouse was not on the same scale as the Wiley's.

"It's nice," Case said when they entered, and he looked around the compact space. There was a kitchenette to his right, a small dining table to his left and the living room was quite roomy. It was decorated in earth tones, chocolate leather sofas, and beige colored curtains. A big screen television was the focal point.

"Two rooms, two bathrooms are upstairs," Lyla said heading for the stairs.

Case followed. She showed him the spaces. Brandi's room was messy; hers was neat.

He smiled at that. "I figured you were a tidy girl," Case said at the door.

Lyla sat on the bed and took off her shoes. "I grew up that way in a place way smaller than this."

Case looked at her longingly. Ideas were streaming through his head. Ideas like, he wasn't honest earlier. He knew exactly what a crush was, when she was describing it, it was as if she was describing his reactions to her to a t.

And then there was the pulsating insidious idea that if they were really married, he would join her on the bed and then he would remove her shoes one by one and then give her a massage. Then he would slowly undress her like the gift she was, and then she would follow suit.

Why on earth had he followed her inside? He was asking for trouble. He was so turned on; he was probably licking his lips…

"Case?" Lyla's husky whisper of his name intruded on his reverie.

"Yes," Case cleared his throat. Who knew what kind of message he was transferring to her just standing there and drinking her in. "I have to go."

Lyla shook her head. "You don't have to."

Case pushed himself from the wall. "I do. Night Lyla."

"Night Case."

He walked down the stairs as if heavy weights were on his feet. Lyla followed him barefooted. At the end of the stairs, he looked back to say goodbye, but the words got stuck in his throat. All he could see was her, all he could smell was her.

She walked into his arms as if he had called her there and they hugged for what felt like hours but was mere minutes. Her curves fit into him just right. She was so tightly pressed to him; he didn't know where she started, and he began.

He was the one who pulled away from her slightly, and he was the one who initiated the kiss.

He fished one hand in her hair, holding her captive to his kiss, while the other swept down along her curves.

He felt as if he couldn't get enough of her, like he was a drowning man, and she was his lifeline. He pulled her even closer to his embrace, so close that he felt the beat of her heart, he heard the soft little moan that broke in her throat as his lips parted hers, and then her arms were around his neck, and she was kissing him back as hungrily as he was kissing her.

This was Lyla. His wife. The girl he had married to give her freedom. If they consummated their relationship, tonight things could get complicated fast.

It took all kinds of control that he didn't know that he had to pull away and whisper raggedly in her ear. "I have to go, Lyla."

She nodded, releasing his shirt reluctantly.

****

He left because he had to. Case sat in his car long after his body had cooled, and his senses had chipped in. Lyla was beginning to mean too much. He thought he was anti-romantic. He thought he was immune to the madness of youth, and the madness of love.

He turned on the radio before he drove off and Wicked Game started playing.

The world was on fire, and no one could save me but you, It's strange what desire will make foolish people do, I'd never dreamed that I'd meet somebody like you…

The radio was reading his mind. He turned it off and drove home in silence.

Chapter Fifteen

The kiss. That's all Lyla thought about for the rest of the week. She wouldn't have minded a replay. She wouldn't have minded if they went further than a kiss. She craved it even, but Case seemed as if he was keeping her at arm's length. She felt like they were in a waltz, two steps forward and one step back.

She wanted to pick his family's brain about it, and she thought she had the chance when she had lunch with Shawn on Wednesday. They ordered food from Yum Yum and sat in the patio area.

Shawn was quite a character; she could sense that immediately.

"I got jealous when I heard you went over to Preston and Sheryl for family dinner," Shawn said when they sat down. "Sheryl said you were a pleasant girl with a sweetness about you that she admired."

"Aw." Lyla grinned. "I like her too."

She also said, she thought that you and Case can go the extra mile. Shawn continued, she poured nearly a tablespoon of pepper while Lyla watched her in horror.

"I have a pepper thing," Shawn said apologetically. "It happened with my last pregnancy, and sure enough it is happening with this one."

"Congratulations." Lyla smiled. "I heard you want a boy."

"Yes." Shawn nodded, "I'll not know for sure until two or so months, it's early days yet."

Lyla ate her food and listened while Shawn prattled on. She was entertaining for sure, but Lyla lit up when Shawn started talking about Portland and her relationship with the brothers.

"I have known them since we were very young," Shawn said. "Jordan's mom, Hannah and my mom, Jackie were very close. They even had a salon together. You should let Case take you to the old place… show you around. Portland is beautiful and quiet."

"We are just friends," Lyla said wryly. "Case doesn't want anything else."

Their kiss had been scorching hot though and had kept her up on Friday night dreaming all sorts of erotic dreams.

"Just friends?" Shawn raised an eyebrow. "He is still running with that ludicrous idea that he will never lose his heart to a woman and that love is just a head thing?"

Lyla nodded.

"Ha," Shawn added more pepper to her food. "Of all the brothers, Case is the one most damaged from his parent's tragic death. He was just five going on six at the time. He was at the house when it happened. The salon was attached to the house. He was probably playing with his cousins in the main house when it happened. I don't know if he saw anything, he probably heard the explosions though. Whatever it is, it weirdly impacted him. I think he associates love with pain and loss and wants nothing to do with it."

"But he loves his brothers and his nieces and nephew." Lyla protested.

"He does." Shawn nodded. "My friend Lacy, who is a psychiatrist might tell you that childhood trauma can have some inexplicable manifestations in adulthood. I was afraid of commitment, and I put Jordan through hell for the better part of our teenage years, and my situation was far different from a boy who witnessed, whether audibly or visually, his parents being gunned down. Not to mention through the years when he was old enough to know that the reason that he had no parents growing up was because of a love triangle."

Lyla sighed.

"Be thankful though," Shawn said cheerily. "He didn't develop any other issues that we know of. Besides, I think that when Case falls, he is going to fall hard."

****

"Hey," Walter stopped by the office she shared with the other interns on Thursday. "Come to my church this weekend and have lunch with us after. I heard that you share a birthday with my brother. That's cause for celebration. You will be included for the birthday party."

"No!" Lyla gasped. "I don't want to intrude."

"Intrude?" Walter shook his head. "No, I don't think so. The more, the merrier. Please email me a list of your friends who you would want to attend."

Lyla stared at Walter in a panic. "I don't think Case would like this."

He had practically blanked her since the kiss.

And probably before that. When she had foolishly told

him that she had a crush and the reality was better than the fantasy. He knew she was talking about him, and he was giving her space.

"This is May," Walter said breezily." By July he'll be singing a different tune."

Lyla doubted that. The week ended and Case had still not called. She went over to the studio and heard that he was unavailable.

"He is locked up in the control room," Jules said balefully. "Working like a beast. He generally leaves here at nine. That's what you get when you decide to do two albums at once. I don't know about this personal project of his."

Jules mumbled and then looked at her. "Want us to have dinner. My new housekeeper has been complaining about me not eating her food. She finds it offensive."

"Sure." Lyla nodded.

"Then come on then," Jules said.

It was not the first time that Lyla was going to Jules' place. Sienna had called it the money pit because Jules had tried to painstakingly restore the main house to reflect the original Georgian design.

It was a large property in the golden triangle of Kingston. For years he had done nothing with it, choosing instead to live out of his suitcase and even renting. But he had finally finished the main house, and he had four cottages that had their own entrances and mini gardens that he had rented out.

It was cute. The landscape was pretty, he had hibiscus plants lining the front of the place, and they were in bloom. Large petals of various colors lined the long driveway.

"Home sweet home." Jules grinned at her. "Finally finished after a decade."

"It's nice." Lyla nodded. "If only Siena could see it."

"She would have lived here with me," Jules said wistfully.

"She would have loved it. Anyway, mi casa is su casa. You can come here at any time. You are like family to me."

Lyla followed him to the kitchen after a walk around the simple yet elegantly decorated house. It had a lot of polished wood that was used for the wainscoting and the ceilings. The kitchen was country chic, with exposed wood beams and white state of the art appliances. It was obviously intended to be the heart of the home.

Lyla remarked as much.

"Pity there will not be the sound of little feet running through here," Jules said wistfully, "I will never have kids."

"Unless you adopt." Lyla reminded him.

"Not alone." Jules shook his head. "I need a help meet."

The helper was still at the house and happy to see them.

The food was good. They ate at the island and talked about Sienna. And Case.

"You know who I've been talking to regularly," Jules said after they had dinner and he gave Lyla a pile of old albums to browse through.

"Who?" Lyla asked looking up from a photograph of a woman who looked so much like her but in period costume. The lady had her face; it was eerie. If she put on a period costume, she could be her.

"Fifi Daniels," Jules said.

"Case's ex?" Lyla raised an eyebrow. "How does he feel about that?"

"I haven't told him," Jules grimaced, "and I doubt it will make a difference. Case does not get jealous like ordinary people. When he does get jealous, I'll know for sure that whoever it is he is jealous over probably has special powers."

The thought of that depressed Lyla. She had half formulated a plan to make Case jealous; it had been brewing at the back of her mind as she tried to figure out how to make him notice her. Make him realize that he had feelings for her.

Now Jules was confirming that playing games like that would be a waste of her time. It was depressing to contemplate. She dragged her mind from that and back to the album.

"Jules, who is this?" She held up the album.

"My great grandaunt Lady Hortense Sienna Greenly," Jules said. "My mom was given her name. I guess because she looks like her."

"And me," Lyla whispered.

"And you." Jules smiled. "She was married to Sir Lionel Greenly, a top man in the government of the day. When she married Sir Lionel, it was scandalous because she was a mixed-race Jamaican woman from the wrong side of the tracks, and he was a privileged white gentleman with royal connections."

"Hortense Greenly," Lyla whistled. "I am going to check her out."

Jules nodded. "If you find anything interesting let me know."

****

It was Friday and Case was still MIA, but Lyla was not dwelling on that. She had a new project, a side project which was even more exciting that the skin care line that they were supposed to be rolling out in a month. Their supervisor from Marketing had them doing intense research. She was supposed to be looking at the competitors and their numbers, checking for costs, but she was busy with the fascinating case of Hortense Greenly.

"So no lunch, huh?" Arthur appeared over her shoulder and then he looked at her screen, and his eyes widened. "Wait a minute, that's you. What was that for, a play?"

"No." Lyla shook her head. "That's not me. This lady was born in the early twentieth century."

"Cool." Arthur pulled up a chair, his eyes lighting up. "I told you it would be rewarding looking for your ancestors."

"She is not my ancestor. Lyla's eyes skittered back to the screen. "She is my former guardian's grandmother."

"And the plot thickens." Arthur raised a brow. "Want to join me at lunch and talk about it?"

"Why not?" Lyla got up. "It is fun to speculate."

And speculate they did. She told Arthur everything about her life including the fact that she was married to Case, and that was why she was Lyla Wiley.

His eyes dimmed a little when he heard that, but he was fascinated with her background.

"So your mother is really Valentina Martinez and the last you heard she was in the States." Arthur steepled his fingers under his chin. "You could find her. It's not hard to find people online. It's a pretty small world now."

"You are probably related to Jules somehow. Maybe from one of his male relatives on this Hortense Greenly's side of the family."

"Wouldn't it be something?" Lyla grinned. "Sienna always said we were blood. Of course, I thought it was just her being eccentric. When she first saw me she claimed that we were connected somehow."

"Interesting." Arthur smiled. "Maybe she was on to something."

They spent most of the lunchtime with their heads bent together doing some online sleuthing. Lyla did not see when Case entered Yum Yum or the fact that the man who did not get jealous was gritting his teeth in irritation when he saw her and Arthur so close.

Chapter Sixteen

"I invited her to church this weekend," Walter said behind him. Case dragged his eyes from Lyla and Arthur.

"Why?" His voice was not working. He sounded a bit too aggressive, even to his own ears.

"Because she is doing the family rounds. Impressing all the Wiley women," Walter said. "Tying you up in knots. Making you feel. I have to get to know her better."

"There is no point," Case said sullenly. "This morning I asked Rita to look into the annulment."

Case had lost his appetite. He walked outside. Even now, Lyla and her new pal hadn't looked up from their screen.

What were they doing? Was it work related? How could it be? Arthur was HR and was only expected to interact with during for orientation.

He felt like marching over to where they were and demand that their heads did not touch or that Arthur brushed her fingers with his.

Why did he care?

Was this what jealousy felt like?

He thrust his hands into his pockets. It had been only five days since he had seen her and already she was moving on. It was what he wanted. She wasn't good for his peace of mind.

She was driving him crazy. In a vain attempt to purge himself of the Lyla effect, he had called Rita and asked her to get the annulment ball a rolling. He would give Lyla the apartment and a decent cash sum and allow her to live her life independently of him. He didn't want to be jealous or be thinking about her every day like and obsessive-compulsive idiot.

"You need to talk to me," Walter said behind him. "Tell me what's going on in that mind of yours."

"Nothing," Case said. "Un-invite her from whatever it is you invited her to. I want a clean break from Lyla related stuff. I don't know why you and the rest of the family have taken it up on your heads to be inclusive to Lyla. She is not a real wife. I am not in love with her. She means nothing to me."

Walter laughed. Big gulping gusts of laughter that had him wiping his eyes when he was done and sniffing.

"Oh, brother." Walter gasped. "I love this."

Case stalked off toward the studio but not before glaring at his brother. "Shut up!"

"You can't tell me to shut up," Walter walked after him, "You have to honor me, that your days may be long upon the land."

Case shook his head. "The fifth commandment says honor your father and mother, not your nosy brother."

Walter grinned. "Just checking that you know your Bible. I am sorry, for laughing earlier. I now know that you'll take out your jealousy on me. I'll not say another word."

"I am not jealous. I am never jealous."

"You know what you should do," Walter said contemplatively, "you should take her out. Stop avoiding her. The more you avoid her, the more she becomes, exotic and untouchable and mysterious in your thoughts."

Case stopped walking abruptly.

Walter actually walked past him and then had to turn back.

"You think that will work?"

"Of course." Walter nodded. "Constant exposure will get rid of the feelings."

"You sure they won't deepen?" Case asked. "I don't want to be in too deep. I never want that for myself. I never want to live that kind of way."

Walter patted him on the back. "I have never met a person who can stop their feelings but try the constant exposure thing and see if it works, huh?"

****

It wasn't working. Case was secretly thinking that Walter had set him up for failure. He had written down certain boundaries he would not cross with Lyla. No kissing. No excessive alone time together. No touching if he could help it. He ended up spending the entire day with her at church—it was easy to follow his rules there.

Lyla charmed Aisha at Walter's after church dinner, and Case resigned himself to another one of his sisters-in-laws liking her.

They spent Sunday at Guy's farm because his brother had insisted on it. Lyla and Lucia got on like a house on fire. Lucia had just done an exhibition in New York and was excited to show them photographs of the pieces because all of her originals were sold out.

Guy took him aside while Lucia and Lyla were talking and whispered to him. "I am glad to see it melting. I think Lyla is worth it."

"What's melting?" Case had asked genuinely confused.

"The ice around your heart and emotions. I knew it would one day. I am just happy that it is with Lyla."

"I am getting an annulment," Case said abruptly. "You are all tripping. Nothing is melting."

****

But something was going on. Guy may have been right. Sandrene went into labor a week later on a Tuesday evening. Saint texted everybody, and he found himself texting Lyla the good news. It was way past nine o'clock and she was already home. He just felt as if he wanted to share that familial milestone with her.

She offered to go to the hospital with him. It was on the way, so he said yes.

On the way there, he looked over at her and how excited she was for his family members, and he realized that Walter had duped him about the feelings fading. They had gotten stronger, but tonight he did not mind it. It was settling with him. He was accepting it. This love thing was not at all bad.

When they drove up to the hospital, it was a crowded waiting room. All his brothers were there including Guy. They didn't comment that Lyla was with him. It felt totally normal.

And that feeling of normality scared him somewhat.

"I remember when Case was being born, we stood in a waiting area just like this, Jordan said to Lyla all misty-eyed. I wanted a little sister, and then my dad came out and said proudly it's another boy, and this one is beautiful. Born with a full head of curly ringlets and long eyelashes like fans, he could be a girl."

"Oh for the love of God," Case said embarrassed. "That's not true."

"Oh yes, it is. Guy nodded. "I remember."

Lyla laughed along with the rest of the brothers.

It was a little after midnight when Saint joined them in the waiting area. "Well, they are here, Sienna and Sarah Wiley, healthy children with a nice set of lungs."

They cheered. They even shared a drink that Walter brought. And he found himself with tears in his eyes when he looked at his nieces, and he didn't bother to blink them away when Lyla joined him.

He was not afraid to be vulnerable around her.

It was something.

Progress.

He thought about that when he dropped her at home.

He thought about that for the following three weeks when they spent most of their waking moments together. It was getting harder and harder to forget his list of don'ts where Lyla was concerned.

He was beginning to see the possibilities of them being together. He was beginning to see the advantages of heart and head love.

****

Four weeks later, Mid-June

They were in the control room. It was a little past nine o'clock. Jules had been the last one to leave. Lyla thought the control room was romantic because of the colorful round lights in the ceiling that gave the space a muted intimate feel.

Lyla was lounging in the leather settee near the piano, while Case tried to add some effects to a tricky track that he was working on all day.

It was hard to concentrate. Lyla was distracting. She was wearing a neat blue suit, and she had hiked up her skirt around her legs to allow for the ease of lounging. She had taken off her shoes and was stretching her toes.

"I need a pedicure," She murmured. A neutral color. "One that won't look awful when the paint begins to chip."

"Your toes look good now," Case responded, looking at her toes and slowly walking his eyes over her creamy skin.

"That is such a guy thing to say," Lyla murmured. "You people of the male sex do not notice the small details."

"We do," Case said seriously. "The ones that matter. Like for instance, I notice that you wear lip gloss and then you chew it off almost immediately.

"I don't chew it off."

"I notice that your skin is smooth and pretty, but you insist on shaving your legs."

"I have to; it's the thing." Lyla sat up straighter in the chair. "I can't leave the house with hairy legs."

"I notice that you wear your hair in buns all the time, even though it looks so good out."

"It's a pain to comb." Lyla chuckled. "I don't have your silky thick curliness. I have to do things to my fine hair to give it volume."

"You don't need makeup."

"That's because you haven't seen me first thing in the morning." Lyla's voice had gotten breathless. "I look bedraggled."

The air between them had thickened with tension.

"First thing in the morning, huh?" Case was looking at her with a kind of limpid intensity that was making her skin prickle.

He got up from the piano and headed for the chair. It was just a few short steps, but the air felt heavy with anticipation.

"I want to kiss you, and I don't know if I'll stop." Case confessed after he sunk down in the seat beside her.

"Why should you stop?" Lyla whispered.

"I don't want to be hurt, Lyla. I am a simple person. I don't want romance and drama and all the flowery, frothy things that people seem to think is required."

"I don't want to be hurt either, Case, and while I am not opposed to over the top public gestures and romance and all of the frothy stuff, I can live without them."

They looked at each other for interminable seconds.

"Lyla," he whispered.

He bent toward her, then hesitated. Lyla didn't think; she was tired of Case hesitating. She was anticipating a situation like this for weeks now. She reached up, clasped his face and brought him to her.

She wanted to communicate. You can trust me with your heart; you don't have to be afraid.

His mouth closed over hers before she could say anything. His kiss was gentle, soft and sweet. But she could feel him trembling, and she knew what was happening. He was fighting to control the need that raged through him because she felt the same thing too.

She hadn't even realized that her blouse was half-off and her hand was tangled in Case's hair when they heard the outer door slam.

It was like a bucket of cold water on both her and Case.

Case dragged his lips from hers and placed his head on hers. His heart was racing and so was hers.

"We are like gun powder and a match."

"Combustible," Case murmured.

"We should take this to your home," Lyla whispered.

"I think we should take this slower."

Lyla groaned in frustration. "I hate your self-control."

"No. This is not self-control." Case shook his head. "This is sheer fear."

Chapter Seventeen

Six weeks. Mid-June

He couldn't remember his life without her in it.

Not to mention the fact that his brothers had accepted her presence in his life. Too well. Case crumpled the paper he was trying to write a song about her on. It was his fiftieth attempt. It was the hardest song he had ever written. He had entitled it, Lyla, and he hadn't gotten past the first line, you changed my mind about love and life…

That sounded too soppy.

Jules knocked on his door and stuck his head in. "You busy?"

"Yes," Case said wryly. "What's up?"

"I was thinking that we should include that duet you did with Lyla on the album."

"What?" Case asked, "Lean on me?"

"That's it." Jules nodded. "I love it. I got the rights. And it sounds better than the solo you did."

Case grinned. "Okay."

"She has a heavenly voice. Jules sat before him. "You did a marvelous thing when you rescued her from her situation in Cuba. You chose the right one. I hope you won't divorce her."

"Annul." Case corrected him.

"Annul?" Jules looked shocked. "With the amount of time you two spend together. I thought you had gone past annul. I thought she was living in your house by now."

Case shook his head. He didn't mention to Jules that after their scorching hot kiss in the control room, they had spent the last two weeks trying not to be alone.

They were combustible. They couldn't get enough of each other. He was finding it harder and harder to resist her. Just yesterday, they had started kissing in the produce aisle. In broad daylight in the Wiley Supermarket.

"She compliments you nicely." Jules picked up one of the crumpled papers and saw that Lyla was scribbled all over the page. Jules looked at him pitifully. What on earth are you waiting on?

"We are still at annul." Case made a face.

Jules laughed. "She looks at you with stars in her eyes."

"You think so?" Case asked leaning back in his chair. Why did that please him so much?

"Yes." Jules nodded vigorously. "Unless of course I need glasses, and I can assure you I don't. I see the way you look at her too."

Case grimaced. "This is the first time I am feeling this way. I am waiting for this thing, whatever it is to pass. It might not last the summer, who knows?"

"Rubbish," Jules said good-naturedly. "With some women, it does not pass. Trust me, I had one night with a girl named Maria, and I still think about her. Two marriages and several women never succeeded in eclipsing her memory."

"Are you sure it wasn't the meal that she cooked?" Case grinned.

"Nah. I am sure," Jules said wistfully. "By the way, have you heard from Fifi Daniels?"

"No." Case shook his head. "Have you?"

"Yes." Jules nodded. "I've been texting her every day. We talk on the phone at night. I see what you saw in her."

"I doubt that." Case sighed. "I wasn't drawn to Fifi like you seem to be drawn to her. She was a sensible choice for me, and I was the man who would have made a difference to her ministry selection committee."

"About that. Jules grimaced. She was outvoted and demoted to a regular minister. I told her to come out here and cool off. She is smarting from the insult."

"I offered her one of my newly renovated cottages to stew in while she figured out what to do next."

Case nodded. "Hello, wife number three."

"I wouldn't rule it out," Jules murmured. "She gives me Maria vibes. I think she could be the final and lasting wife."

"Oh for goodness sakes, at least get to know her first," Case said, "you are half the reason why I am so cautious with relationships."

"I'll do that." Jules grinned. "By the way, I saw Lyla with what's his name at Yum Yum. You should go show up."

"I am not a stalker. It is probably totally innocent." Case got up slowly. "On the other hand, I am hungry."

"Can I just say," Jules grinned at him, "you have never written a song about a woman before. It is nice to see you so flustered."

"Oh shut up."

"And in denial," Jules said and left the office laughing.

Case headed for Yum Yum Cafe. It was a little before

lunchtime, Lyla had already said that she couldn't dine with him today. She was going to be swamped with work, and yet she was there with Arthur.

It was stupid how jealous he felt. He was halfway across the parking lot before he realized that he was on the verge of stalking her.

Stalking. Spying. Checking on. Torture. That was what this love business did to people.

He didn't like how out of control he felt, how suspicious he was acting.

He despised it. He turned around and headed back to the office. He needed to do something about this madness.

"Case!" Brandi was in the parking lot. She spotted him before he could make it all the way.

"How are you these days?" Brandi grinned at him. "Did I tell you I like working here? Are you heading to lunch? Me too. I love Yum Yum food. Come on then."

He was swept toward Yum Yum by Brandi who did not wait for an answer.

****

"Lyla I barely see you these days at lunch time." Arthur folded his arms in front of him. "It's no secret that you spend most of your lunchtimes with Case, and I hear that you are getting your vocal cords tested at the studio."

Lyla smiled. "That's true."

"How is the side singing career coming on?" Arthur grinned at her.

"I enjoy it." Lyla rested back in her chair.

"Have you wondered where you got the talent from?" Arthur asked leaning forward. "Was it your mother or father?"

"I don't know. Haven't given the genealogy a thought since we researched Valentina Martinez and ended up with nothing. I was thinking of quitting the research. Let sleeping dogs lie."

"I have thought about it." Arthur picked up a gift bag that was beside him, "and I have something for you."

Lyla could see the words Know Your Roots, DNA testing kit at the top of the box.

"This is where I did mine," Arthur said helpfully. "They have a wide database. I think they share data with other places."

"Oh Arthur, you shouldn't have," Lyla said. Pulling out the box and belying her eagerness to examine the kit.

"Everybody should know their roots, and I am curious on your behalf. I am a stickler for puzzles, why do you look like Jules? Who was Valentina Martinez?" Arthur tapped the box. "The test is simple. Just a swipe of the inside of your mouth. Seal the container, when you are done. If you do it by tonight, I can ask Winston to take it to the States with him. He is leaving tomorrow evening. You should get your results in fourteen days or earlier."

"That easy, huh?" Lyla looked at the gift fearfully.

"Just do it." Arthur gave her a little salute. "You'll thank me later, and get Jules to take the test as well."

Lyla gave him a warm smile and reached over and kissed his cheek. "Thank you for your curiosity and for caring."

Arthur grinned. "No problem. What do you want for lunch?"

"I was thinking of having lunch at my desk." Lyla made a face. "I have real piles of work to get through, uh."

"Okay then. Arthur nodded. I am going to get something to eat."

"Oh look, there is Case. I imagine your plans will be

canceled now."

Lyla spun around and saw Case and Brandi in the main café looking at them through the window.

Case said something to Brandi and then left.

Lyla groaned. His expression had been stormy. Her first instinct was to race after him and explain, and she got up to do it, but Brandi came up to her and whispered fiercely what are you doing trying to make Case jealous.

Lyla smiled. "You think he was jealous?"

"As I've ever seen," Brandi widened her eyes. "He may head back to the office and break something. Why are you smiling?"

"If Case is jealous, that means he feels something!

"I never know for sure what he is thinking. Jealousy is progress."

Brandi snorted. "Don't poke the bear, what were you talking to Arthur about?"

"DNA," Lyla said smugly and then went on to explain.

****

Case fumed all the way to the studio after seeing Lyla with Arthur. She had kissed him on the cheek. She had casually reached over and kissed Arthur Jones on his cheek.

He was not jealous. He was not possessive.

Nope, he wasn't.

He was feeling sick to his stomach. Maybe it was something he had for breakfast.

Lyla could talk to anyone she wanted. She was a free agent. She could kiss all the boys she wanted. He had married her with the intention to let her go anyway. He had lost sight of that over these last couple of weeks.

A little part of him had thought that they had the beginnings of something lasting. He had been wrong. It was what he had expected when he decided to pursue a relationship with something other than his head.

These were the sort of things that came with the territory, and he had had enough. Staying up all night and thinking about one girl, feeling his heart pound when she came into the same room was obviously a fool's game. He needed to go back to how he viewed life before Lyla came casually strolling into his. She had the potential to hurt him, and he was not going to have that.

He tried to practice hardening his heart against her. It wasn't hard. He got engrossed in the production of the background music for one of the songs on a Case of Love. It was a tricky sound and required all of his concentration.

He didn't realize that it was after six and that he was hungry until Jules came into the live room.

"Hey, Lyla just brought us food."

Case took off his headphones and frowned. "Not hungry."

"You didn't eat lunch," Jules smirked. "And it is Fish from Freddy's."

Case was almost moved. He loved Freddy's fish. She knew that. This was probably her apology gift for dating Arthur and getting caught.

"You two had a fight?" Jules asked.

"No." Case grimaced. "We are just friends. I'd forgotten that. That's all.

Arthur gave her a DNA testing kit at lunch today as a gift. Apparently, he is a DNA fanatic or something. She kissed him on his cheek to show her appreciation. You saw them at the same time. End of story."

Case wrinkled his brow. "She told you this?"

"Yep," Jules said. "It is a testing kit for two. She asked me if I wanted to do the other one."

Case stood up. "Are you?"

Jules made a face. "I don't know. You think I should?"

"Why not?" Case asked. "It can't hurt. Maybe you two are related. It wouldn't hurt to find out.

"I couldn't process it." Jules shook his head. "It would be amazing. She is a great girl. My mother should be alive to see this if she is really family."

"Yes." Case ran his fingers through the long hair at the top of his head.

"Are you over your jealousy now that you know the truth?" Jules asked shrewdly. "Lyla wanted to know. She is anxious about your response."

"I don't do jealous." Case growled. "I'll never be jealous over anyone. See, you started something with Fifi. It doesn't bother me."

"But you don't feel for Fifi like you do Lyla," Jules said patiently. "You love her, don't you? You have certainly been acting like it."

"I don't know what love is." Case growled. "I called Rita today, told her that I wanted the annulment. I am better off alone."

Then he heard a gasp. Lyla was at the door; her face looked stricken as if he had dealt her a blow.

If he had an extra foot, he would kick himself. He did know what love was and he had been jealous. Terribly jealous. He had never experienced such dark emotions before. His ego was getting in the way, and it felt as if he couldn't stop himself.

"Listen Lyla," he started but didn't know why his voice went all husky and quivery. "I am sorry, but I think we should get that annulment. Move on."

"And then you'll do what?" Lyla squinted at him, "be safe from your emotions?"

"Something like that." Case nodded. It was his only moment of honesty since he denied that he was jealous, and he didn't love her.

"Fine," Lyla said slowly and deliberately. "When you get us annulled, you don't owe me anything. I don't want your apartment or your money. I'll get by. I don't want you to feel as if you are obligated to me anymore. You have been great. Perfect actually. Maybe that is why I like you in the first place. Maybe I should find someone, anyone other than you to invest some emotions into."

"Wait a minute." Case swallowed nervously. "No, I…"

"As a matter of fact," Lyla's eyes were sparkling with tears, "I'll move out tonight."

"And where will you go?" Case asked fearfully. "Lyla this is an overreaction."

"She'll come by me of course," Jules interjected. "Right Lyla? Mi casa is su casa."

Lyla glared at Case and then turned to Jules. "Sure, I'll stay by you."

Case opened his mouth and then closed it. "Fine, do whatever!"

"I will!" Lyla yelled, storming out of the building in a rage; he heard all the outer doors being slammed and a car squealing out of the parking lot.

"Your first quarrel as married folks," Jules said rubbing his hands together. "Don't worry about it. It's just growing pains every couple goes through it. Excuse me, I have to call the housekeeper to prepare a room and send my driver to pick up Fifi from the airport."

Jules guffawed. "Seems as if I'll be hosting your exes under my roof. This should be fun."

Chapter Eighteen

Fifteen days without Case and life moved on. She felt bereft and lonely as if they were in each other's lives for far longer than that six and a half weeks. She had gotten the annulment papers by courier earlier in the day. She had sat and looked at it as if it were poisonous. That was when Walter had found her.

"Hey, party next week," Walter said smiling. He dropped off her invitation, and she had not bothered to open it until the evening.

When she did, she saw that the invitation said: you are cordially invited to the Wiley Cluster Party. Jordan Wiley will be 34, Lyla Wiley will be 21, and Aisha Wiley is having a gender reveal. All day event at Guy Wiley's Strawberry Farm.

Walter was so thorough he had included a map to the farm, dress code and menu.

He obviously had not heard that Case had blanked her. Her

annulment papers were here. She was soon to go back to being Lyla Martinez. She was sure that Case didn't want her using his name.

"Walter, wait!" Lyla got up and hurried after Walter. "Haven't you heard? Case and I are over. I just got the annulment papers today!"

"Yep," Walter nodded. "But surely you are not going to sign, are you?"

"Yes," Lyla hissed. "It is what Case wants. He can't wait to get rid of me."

Walter stood at the elevator and then turned to her. "He said you moved out."

"Yes," Lyla nodded. "I am doing fine on my own. I don't need Case."

"Jules said he hears you crying at night." Walter raised an eyebrow. "Phillip from my office said he asked you out and you shrieked, no."

"I am not interested in Phillip. I am not interested in anyone, and why is Jules reporting to you. I am not crying. I have allergies. I sneeze, and I sniffle. There is something about his house that is irritating me."

Walter chuckled.

"I hope he isn't reporting the same thing to Case. I am through with being the person of pity, the one who always needs help. I am making an independent stand."

"And I admire that." Walter nodded, "but have you ever thought about it, at some point or the other we all need help. And Case does not see you as a person of pity."

"Just a person who he can't love," Lyla said weakly. It got to her every time she thought about it. Case didn't love her. He hadn't loved Fifi who he had asked to marry him. Maybe he couldn't love anyone.

"Case is pining away; he is locked up in the studio writing

songs and feeling sorry for himself." Walter shook his head. "He growls when we ask him about you. He has this impression that you are living a party lifestyle and you are dating all the guys in the building, and he is noble and good for setting you free."

"Where would he get that impression?" Lyla widened her eyes.

"I have no clue." Walter punched the elevator button and looked at her knowingly. "Maybe Jules. I figure he is trying to gaslight Case into action."

"But that's wrong," Lyla whispered. "I don't want Case to think those things about me."

The elevator door opened, and a bearer stepped out and headed to the reception desk.

Walter held the door. "The family is rooting for the two of you to work out. It is obvious that you two need to talk."

"I am not going to beg Case Wiley to love me," Lyla whispered. "He doesn't love me, and I am not going to be pathetic and beg him to. We can't work if he doesn't love me."

Walter nodded. "I hear you, but you love him, right?"

"Right." Lyla inhaled shakily. "Since I was a fourteen-year-old girl. I am pathetic."

"No, not pathetic." Walter smiled at her, "It's never pathetic when you love someone. Stay positive, Lyla."

He stepped into the elevator, and the receptionist called to her when she turned around

"Lyla Wiley, there is a package here for you."

Lyla went over to the desk and wondered vaguely what on earth could be next. She was served with annulment papers. What's next, a note to evacuate the premises?

It was a manila envelope that was marked private and confidential, and it was from Know Your Roots.

She took the package without much enthusiasm and walked toward the office.

****

Lyla looked longingly across the parking lot at Wiley Studios before she got in her car. It was a little after seven. She was seriously considering going back to the apartment, Brandi had texted her and asked her when she was coming back. She was tempted.

Especially after Rita called her.

"Did you get the papers?" Rita asked after the pleasantries.

"Yes, I did." Lyla stopped in the yard and picked up her briefcase.

"They are pretty straight forward." Rita continued. "Case wanted me to tell you that the house, the car, the bank account, they are all yours. Staying at Jules is not cool. His words, not mine," Rita said hurriedly.

Lyla chuckled. "Yes, I hear you."

She hung up from Rita and left the car. All the kitchen lights were on so Jules was home. It would be nice to open the DNA test with him. They could have a good laugh. She could go on the site and check to see if they had found any family members of hers and then they could call it a night.

She was shocked to see Fifi Daniels sitting on a bar stool. She had not seen Fifi for the two weeks she was in Jamaica. She had holed up herself in the cottage and only communicated with Jules.

"Oh hey," Lyla said awkwardly.

Fifi was looking down in her tea mug. She raised her head and looked at Lyla barely cracking a smile. "You look professional."

"I am just getting home from work." Lyla put her briefcase

on the bar stool beside her and looked around. "Where is Jules?"

"Gone to change. He convinced me to go out." Fifi sighed. "I just decided to join the land of the living. I did a twelve day fast and I prayed. I think I know what is next for me now."

"I see." Lyla nodded. She didn't see though. It was obvious that Fifi was depressed and she had lost a ton of weight. She appeared gaunt. Her hair was in disarray like she had just pulled it back into a ponytail without much care, wisps of hair were hanging around her face.

"No, you don't see." Fifi sighed. "You were one reason why I was locked up in the cottage. Jules never said you were staying here when I arrived."

"I am not interested in Jules," Lyla protested. "You don't have to worry about me. I am going to leave soon anyway."

Fifi fanned her off. "I don't like children. Usually, when I say that people looked shocked. I have stopped saying it out loud in public."

Lyla gasped. Was Fifi Daniels inferring that she was a child?

"I am not talking about you." Fifi said, "I like you quite a bit."

"Well thanks, I guess." Lyla wanted to leave. Fifi was acting weird. Almost drunk.

"I went to Cuba," Fifi inhaled raggedly, "saw my parents. They are old now and weak. They live near Hemingway House. You know there?"

"Yes." Lyla nodded. "I know Finca Vigia quite well."

Fifi sighed. "You know Case likes cats, like Hemingway?"

Lyla nodded and started to get up. "Well, I need to go to my room and unwind."

"No, don't leave." Fifi had tears in her eyes. "I need to talk.

I lost my husband. I lost my fiancé, and I lost my ministry. It is gone. I sold my soul for twenty pieces of silver, and I lost it all."

Lyla sat back down in her chair, and she heard Jules coming. Well, she smelled him first he must have bathed in perfume.

Fifi sounded as if she had an interesting story to tell. Maybe she could tell him. She was slightly under the weather herself. Somehow, she didn't want to hear Fifi's sob story. Where was her compassion?

She had run out, it seemed.

"Say, Fifi," Jules came into the kitchen with a stack of menus in hand. "If you don't feel like going out, we can eat in. I have a wide range of options to choose from."

He looked at Lyla and grinned. "Hey."

"Hey." Lyla smiled. She had to, Jules was dressed to the nines in navy blue shirt, an obviously expensive denim pants and matching navy shoes. He looked good.

All of this was for Fifi, but Fifi barely glanced at him. She had her head back down in her mug. She was really depressed.

"I am not hungry," Fifi said, "I can't eat food when I am just coming off a fast. I had a vegetable broth instead. It was delicious the most delicious broth I have ever eaten."

Jules looked at Fifi tenderly. "Well then, it's just up to me and Lyla."

"Not hungry either," Lyla muttered. "I think I am going to my room. I am moving back to my place tomorrow."

"Why?" Jules asked. "Is it something I did?"

"No." Lyla shook her head. "Rita asked me to, and don't you think it is ridiculous that I moved out of the house, but I still drive the car. Case bought all of that for me. If I were really going independent, I would ditch everything and go it alone.

"Oh, by the way, got the DNA results, didn't even open it today."

"Let us hear it." Jules rubbed his hands together. "Maybe we are related like a 2% or something."

Fifi sat up straighter in her chair and was looking over at Lyla interestedly too.

"Okay," Lyla grinned at both of them. "Let's see," she pulled the package out of the briefcase and opened it.

There were two papers in there, a paternity report and the relationship report. She held up the one with the title DNA Paternity Report and scanned the columns, there was her name, and there was Jules' name and then she saw the probability of paternity, 99.999%. There were so many nines after the .9999 she didn't bother to count them.

"What does it say?" Fifi was the one who asked her urgently.

"It says that Based on the analysis of STR loci listed above, the probability of paternity is 99.99999999% "

Jules was shaking his head. "Say what?"

Lyla giggled nervously.

"I know you are playing." Jules grinned. "For a while there you had me."

Lyla shook her head and handed him the paper.

Jules looked it over and then sat down hard on one of the bar stools. "I can't believe it. I just can't."

"The question is daddy, who is my mommy?" Lyla sat down beside him.

****

"I just can't," Jules murmured over and over again. "This can't be."

"They say DNA don't lie," Fifi murmured. "You are the father, Raphael."

Jules got up and started pacing. Lyla watched him in a daze. This was her father. Julius. Raphael Julius Harvey. The good for nothing tourist that Consuela always harped on about. The only clue she had ever had about her father.

She didn't know how to feel. It hadn't sunk in yet.

She ran through the rest of the information while Jules paced and then got the information for her special login on the site.

She wanted to see her family tree. The paper said she had hundreds of relationship matches.

"What are you doing?" Fifi asked her sharply when she took out her laptop.

"Checking my other relatives," Lyla said. "I have a ton of them on both sides of my family tree. Maybe I can even find my mother on here."

"That's funny," Fifi said without any discernible expression at all, "because your mother is right here."

Chapter Nineteen

It was a bombshell. It detonated in the kitchen with a bang. Obviously, the night was full of shocks. Lyla heard a small sound it was from Jules. He looked as if he was gasping for breath.

"I guess I have a story to tell." Fifi massaged her temples. "I guess I better start from the beginning. I was born in Havana Cuba to Raul and Consuela Martinez, two of the most toxic people you could ever find. They were bad together. I was born on Valentine's Day, so of course, I was called Valentina. My middle name was Maria. By the time I was nine my dad had left us, he died a couple of months after that. By the time I was eleven, my mom tried to sell me."

Lyla gasped. "Oh my goodness."

"I had an asthma attack the very same day and was rushed to the hospital. I told the doctors my story, and they sent me to a place of safety, aka the orphanage. A year later, I was adopted by the Lopez family and was renamed Fifi which means may Jehovah add. Sounds treacly sweet and touching doesn't it?

"When I was sixteen papa Lopez decided that I should replace his wife in his bed."

Fifi winced. "That was my first pregnancy. I lost the baby and ran away from my 'loving' home. I found my sister who was a dancer at a nightclub, and she got me a job. I was there for a year when I met this Jamaican student named Raphael."

Jules' eyes got wider and wider, the more Fifi unfolded her story.

"I had a one-night stand with Raphael. I thought I was in love."

"You cooked me vaca frita," Jules whispered. "It's really you. I can't believe this."

Fifi laughed dryly without humor. "The evening after the one-night stand, Papa Lopez spotted me at the club. Started harassing me to come home. I had to leave the premises. So I went right back to my biological mother. Consuela Martinez, the one person in the world who I shouldn't have gone back to. I had no choice. I had nowhere else to go. I found out I was pregnant two months later. This time I had the baby, a beautiful little girl, I named her Lyla."

"Me?" Lyla whispered. "Is this true?"

"Oh yes." Fifi was determined to get on with her story as emotionlessly as possible. "I am the ingrate who left you with Consuela. I had to do it, you see. I had to escape. When you were born Consuela worked at a restaurant, and she had this customer she was trying to woo. He was a minister from America. She saw dollar signs. We rarely got American visitors. Cuba was different then.

"Anyway, Consuela was trying to sell herself as a pious woman who had not a peso to rub together, but he wasn't interested. Until she spun him a sob story about her two orphaned girls and how hard she had it. She spun a tale about how innocent her older girl was, and how she wanted to preserve my innocence because all the boys on the block wanted me.

"It aroused his protective instincts. He met me, and he fell in love with me. We got married and one year later. I was out of Cuba. He thought that the baby was Consuela's. He thought I was an innocent girl that was as pure as the driven snow. I couldn't tell him otherwise when I moved with him to America, so I left you. Pretended that you were my sister."

Jules made a choking sound.

"I acted for eighteen years." Fifi sighed. "Someone should give me an Oscar."

"You left Lyla with your mother. Nobody should you give you anything." Jules hissed. "You are a selfish person. You abandoned your own child to a mother who you knew was not the best and yet you are asking for a medal?"

"I know I am selfish," Fifi growled. "I wanted to escape Cuba and all of the unpleasantness behind. I would have married a horse. I was that desperate. I couldn't tell my husband the truth and blow my cover. The Bishop would not have been very forgiving.

"I wasn't totally absent either. I paid Consuela to take care of Lyla. She was supposed to take care of Lyla and not be the beast she was to me."

"And what about when your husband died?" Jules asked incredulously. "Why didn't you get in touch?"

"I was the head of a popular ministry." Fifi shrugged, "Announcing a daughter out of nowhere would have been a shock I am not sure my people could have dealt with."

"You mean you didn't want the world to know about your past before you developed your Evangelist Fifi persona!" Jules said angrily.

"You are not without fault, Jules. You slept with anybody in a skirt, and you didn't think that for one moment you would get someone pregnant."

"I thought I was sterile!" Jules screeched. "I was treated for cancer shortly after you!"

"Well, both of us are to blame," Fifi said passionately. "I didn't contribute to her genetic makeup alone."

Lyla looked from Jules to Fifi. They were just getting started. They were playing the blame game with each other. She wondered what it would be like to have grown up with both of them or, even one of them. She was stumped.

If she had stayed with Jules, she would have had Sienna for a longer time. That would be a positive. If she had stayed with Fifi, what would it have been like? She couldn't picture it. She didn't know Fifi that well.

"Listen, it may have been wrong when I left it all behind, but I did it. The truth is, I was planning to go to Cuba to face what I had done after Barbados but imagine my surprise when I met not only my daughter but her father in Barbados. One was married to my fiancé, and the other was his manager. You can't make this stuff up."

Jules shook his head. "I can't believe this is my life. I saw my own child in Cuba and would have passed her by if Case had not insisted that he help. It's Case why we are even having this conversation! I would have passed my own flesh and blood. Your mother had her in a state. We owe Case."

Fifi sighed loudly. "I know."

"No, I don't think you understand," Jules said passionately, he spent his resources, and he took care of Lyla when he didn't have to. He paid for her education; he pays for her food, clothing and shelter and protection. We were on tour in Africa when Rita, his lawyer, told him that there were some robberies going on in the area where she lived. My mother was in the hospital at the time, so he told Rita to buy a house for Lyla in a secure area.

"Buy a house! You know what I said?" Jules asked hoarsely, "I teased him that he cared too much for a girl he didn't even know, and it was a bad investment. I was the one who should have been concerned."

Lyla had never heard the story. She stared at Jules, her eyes opened wide. "He never told me that."

"He wouldn't," Jules sighed. "He treated you better in absentia that a lot of men treated their wives even though he was just a young man himself. I can't begin to repay him."

Fifi started to sob. "I am so sorry, Lyla. Please forgive me."

Lyla looked from Fifi to Jules. "It's okay. I don't regret how I came to be at this point in my life. If it's forgiveness you both want. Done."

Fifi sniffed. "Thank you. I went back to Cuba, faced my adopted parents, and I forgave them. Then I faced Consuela. She is much the same as before. She said you ran away, Lyla, and she didn't know where you were."

Lyla nodded. "Consuela will be Consuela."

Fifi sighed. "I am afraid she is much the same and has no intention of changing."

"I don't know what to say," Jules murmured. "This is too much. Really too much."

"I know." Fifi looked at Lyla. "I hope I haven't shocked you much. I want to start a relationship with you Lyla."

That was when it sunk in. Fifi Daniels was her mother. Jules Harvey was her father. And even though she knew that she had a family now. The family she had always prayed that she could have but at the back of her mind was the niggling thought that she wanted to stay Lyla Wiley forever.

She loved Case. There would be no other man on the planet for her but him, and if she had to grovel to get him back and if she had to convince him that it was okay to love her, she would never hurt him, she would.

She would be loyal for life.

"I would like some time to sort this all out in my head," Lyla murmured. "Excuse me. I am going upstairs."

****

Ain't no sunshine when she's gone, only darkness every day…Case was listening to Bill Withers on surround sound at his home studio. The place was soundproofed, and he was glad for that. He glanced at his phone that was vibrating and saw the name Lyla on his screen.

The magical name. The only name he had wanted to see.

He quickly grabbed the phone from the table. If she hadn't called, he would have. He was beginning to believe that Aint No Sunshine When She's Gone was written for him.

"Hey," he said quickly.

"Hey," Her voice was husky and sounded wobbly as if she was crying. "I got the papers today."

He groaned inwardly. He had forgotten about them, until today when Rita had called. In his quest to finish the album and try not to think about her, he had allowed himself to forget, but he sensed that was not the only thing wrong with her.

"What's wrong?" He asked urgently.

"Fifi Daniels is my mother!" Lyla whispered. "Jules is my father! They are my biological parents, which means that Sienna was my grandmother. My real grandmother and all the dusty photos of the ancestors that Jules has saved I am related to them."

"Hold up." Case sat up straighter in the couch. "Explain."

She ran through the whole scenario, and he was literally

stunned. "I thought that you might be related to Jules but not in a million years, Fifi."

Case looked at the clock. "Want us to talk face to face? You sound like you could use a friend."

"I…I …could." Lyla sighed. "They are still downstairs. I don't want to talk to any of them right now. They are arguing about which one of them is the worst. I think a lot of that is guilt. Especially Jules. He claims you took over his responsibilities."

"Come over," Case said huskily, "you never got the house tour."

She dithered over the invitation and that made Case grit his teeth. She was gearing up to say no.

When she finally sighed and said, "Okay," he couldn't believe it.

****

Lyla drove up to Case's house. Before she could get out of the car he was at the door, in a grey tracksuit, his hair tousled, looking adorable. Why did she agree to come tonight? She had called him because she wanted to talk. She didn't know anybody else who would understand the shock she was going through.

She thought he would appreciate the irony that the girl he rescued was the daughter of two people he was familiar with—that and the fact that she had wanted an excuse to call him.

She loved Case.

She looked at him standing at his door as he watched her as she headed for him and her heart swelled with it. He was not just handsome; he had a good heart.

A heart that was resisting her because he thought that he

should give her freedom or something like that.

She walked up to him, and he opened his arms. She went into them. She was home, and she never wanted to leave.

Case gave her the tour of his place, and it was exactly how she would imagine that it would be. His place was monochrome with splashes of red. Every room was coordinated professionally.

They ended up on the patio. They sat in lounge chairs beside each other.

Ferb and Phin came over to tell her hello. When they finished sniffing her, they curled up beside Case.

"I was listening to Aint No Sunshine, and when you called." Case laughed depreciatingly, "I missed you."

He reached across the chair and squeezed her hand.

"I missed you too." Lyla turned her head and looked at him. "So what did you do while you were hiding from me?"

"Almost finished an album." Case grinned, "the small pain I felt in my heart from your absence added another dimension to my music. My personal album is going to be on another level."

Lyla chuckled. "Well, at least I was good for something."

Case laced his fingers with hers. "I wrote a song for you."

"Oh really?" Lyla widened her eyes. "Is it good?"

"It is, I think," Case murmured. "Enough about me, tell me how you are feeling about Fifi and Jules."

"I like Jules, I have always liked him." Lyla sighed. "I guess one day; eventually, I'll start thinking of him as a father. As for Fifi, she says she wants to get to know me. I am fine with that. I am so happy that you didn't marry her."

Case chuckled. "Me too."

"She seems depressed," Lyla murmured. "She said she lost her ministry. They are replacing her on her television show with Cory Daniels, and she is going to have to start from scratch."

Case nodded. "I feel sympathy for her. It's not easy starting over."

They talked way up into the night.

Lyla left after one and decided to head to her apartment. She didn't want to face Jules and Fifi quite yet.

Chapter Twenty

Lyla overslept the next morning and was awakened by a shocked Brandi who couldn't believe that she was home again.

When she blinked up at Brandi, she was already dressed.

"You are going to be late." Brandi declared. "And today is a huge day. We are doing focus groups. I can't wait to see what the group says."

"I forgot about it." Lyla groaned.

"Better hurry up. Brandi turned to the door. "We will be in Conference Room One, while we watch the group in Conference Room Two."

"Okay." Lyla jumped out of bed. "I'll be there in record time."

"So since you are back here, does this mean that you and Case are back together again? Brandi asked curiously.

"Maybe, I am not sure." Lyla giggled. "He said he had a surprise for me today and he wrote a song for me. That has to count for something."

"Aw." Brandi chuckled. "Good for you, I am rooting for you and Case. Anyway, bye. I hear my phone ringing; Adam is probably downstairs."

Lyla did everything in record time. She couldn't even focus on her late-night conversation with Case and how they had hot chocolate in the wee hours and found a million and one things to talk about.

And she definitely didn't have time to think about Jules and Fifi and how the two of them were parents.

She arrived at work fifteen minutes later than usual, and already the day felt like it was going at breakneck speed.

Her lunch break couldn't come soon enough, but she made it a point of duty to stay behind and collate the findings from their focus group sessions. She hadn't missed the fact that Case was in the building in Conference Room Two, with his brothers. They were huddled over some paperwork or the other.

They looked busy. At least Case had given her a small wave when he walked in. Preston had on his no-nonsense face, and he had drawn the blinds after it seemed as if they were in a heated discussion.

She was in the middle of putting the questionnaires together when the conference room phone rang. It was for her.

Fifi Daniels was here to see her, said the receptionist.

Lyla grimaced. She had not expected Fifi to visit her at work.

"Send her to Conference Room Two," Lyla said absentmindedly.

When Fifi was shown in, she was dressed to the nines in a pink suit. It was obviously expensive. Her hair was sleekly coifed, and she looked nothing like the downtrodden woman from yesterday.

"I thought you would return home last night," Fifi said after hugging her briefly. "But in your absence, Jules and I got a chance to talk about the hard stuff. Called each other names. Aired out all our grievances."

Lyla nodded. "I guess you guys needed that."

"We did." Fifi nodded. "We are friends again. I hope as time goes by, we will be even more. If it is God's will."

Lyla grinned. "My mother and father together, like a real family. That should be interesting."

"After we aired our grievances," Fifi cleared her throat, "we started talking about you."

"Okay." Lyla nodded.

"Jules said you got annulment papers from Case."

Lyla nodded absently. "I did."

"I have money; my husband died leaving me a wealthy woman," Fifi said briskly. "Jules has money; you are his only child. In fact, this morning we are meeting lawyers to change our wills. You never have to worry about your schooling again or depend on Case again. He did his part; Jules and I will pay him back every dime."

"What?" Lyla snapped up her head and brushed the pile of papers she was stacking half slipped off the pile.

"You were helpless and alone in this world, but now we are here. We can help," Fifi said calmly. "You should sign those papers. Live free."

"No." Lyla shook her head, "I don't want to be free of Case. I love him. I feel as if I have loved him forever."

"This is your get out of jail free card, Lyla," Fifi insisted. "You probably think you love Case because he has been all you know. You need to expand your wings, live a little."

"I don't want to know anyone else," Lyla gritted out. "I know what I want, and Case is it. I don't want anyone else! I'll never want anyone else. I have made up my mind. I would love Case if he were broke and begging off the street and if he couldn't sing another note. Please leave, I have work to do."

Fifi got up and came over to her and unexpectedly hugged her. "Well then, I dearly hope Case loves you back because I want the absolute best for you, Lyla."

Lyla hugged her back, "Thank you, Fifi. I hope so too."

"If he doesn't, he has me to contend with. Belatedly, but I am here." Fifi stepped away, "Say, can you come to dinner later? I am cooking vaca frita."

Lyla nodded. "Yes, I will, can I take a date?"

"Yes, Case is invited too." Fifi nodded. "The more, the merrier."

****

Case and his brothers watched the screen in Conference Room One silently. Somebody had forgotten to turn off the video feed from that room. It had been the focus group room.

They had been in the middle of voting for a new business venture when Fifi had walked into the room, and they heard the conversation.

When Fifi walked out, they looked at each other in disbelief.

Saint cleared his throat. "Fifi is her mother?"

Guy shook his head. "Forget that. You can't let Lyla go, Case. She is the real deal."

"Yes, she is." Preston smiled. "What a wonderful girl."

"Imagine, she doesn't know we are watching, does she?" Jordan murmured. "She just declared her love for Case like a boss."

"That was a real, raw moment," Saint said. "She got the opportunity to ditch you, and she was having none of it."

"What I want to know is," Walter as grinning from ear to

ear, "are you two going to have a real wedding ceremony this time? So that we can all be there cheering you on."

Case grinned. "First I am going to tell the lady that I love her, then I'll propose for real and if she says yes, we'll have the wedding."

"You should make it grand," Walter said. "Make it huge! She just declared her feelings for you in no uncertain terms. You should do the same for her."

"I am not into those kinds of things, Walter." Case dismissed his brother. "Grand gestures are not my thing. I have an interview shortly to plug my personal album. Can we please speed this up?"

****

Lyla was feeling half sleep by the time five o'clock rolled around. She was half leaning in the elevator when Arthur entered.

"Lyla!" He smiled at her, how is it going?

Lyla grinned. "You won't believe this. I found both my mother and my father, and they were right under my nose."

"Really?" Arthur said excitedly. "Tell me more."

"I will." Lyla yawned, "but it is a long story, maybe some other time. I have a dinner date."

When they exited into the lobby, the big screen televisions both had on an interview with Case.

He was talking to the interviewer.

She stopped. "This must be about his new personal album."

Arthur stopped behind her. "I can't wait to hear it. I am a C Wiley fan myself."

A small crowd was gathered around the first television a bigger one at the second. Brandi spotted her in the smaller crowd and gestured for her to come near. "He is debuting his new single live."

"Oh, he didn't say he would do that today." Lyla moved closer.

"I dedicate this one to my wife," Case said to the interviewer. "The song is about her; I called it For Lyla."

"Your wife?" The interviewer looked shocked. "C. Wiley is married?"

"Yes, I am." Case grinned into the camera. "She's the one, and I love her."

"I just heard a million groans around the world." The interviewer grinned. "Anyway, I cannot be the only one anxious to hear a non-gospel single from C. Wiley. So let's have it."

Case got up and he sung:

Lyla I just want to tell you that whatever you do, never stop being you,

I sense that together we'll make a hell of a team, despite my stubbornness a man can dream,

And so I'll present my argument, I never believed in romance or the messy bits of love,

But I prayed about this, I asked my friend above,

And you know what the verdict was my island girl, this is a Case of Love.

They cheered in the lobby when he was finished singing. It was a beautiful song. He had a beautiful voice.

"This one is a hit!" The interviewer said excitedly, "absolutely lovely!"

Lyla had tears in her eyes when he was done. She wiped them away, and when she looked around, he was there.

"The program is not live." He grinned at her. "I was over there watching you, while you listened." He pointed to a corner of the lobby.

Lyla sniffed. "I loved the song. I mean as grand romantic gestures go. This one was over the top."

"Not yet, the grand romantic gesture begins now." Case got down on one knee, in the lobby, with all the people around.

There was a hush when he did it. All eyes were on them.

"Lyla, I love you, every piece of me loves you. Will you marry me, again? For real this time."

"Yes!" Lyla squealed.

She didn't hear the cheers around her or saw that the rest of the Wiley brothers and Jules and nearly all the staff from Wiley studios was around them. She kneeled down beside Case and kissed him.

Epilogue

Three months later

It was the largest Wiley wedding to date. The bride looked like a fairy tale bride in her princess wedding gown, the groom sang her song, For Lyla, when she walked down the aisle. On her side of the church was almost as packed as his with her newly discovered family members.

They remarried in Portland in the parish church. Pete was his best man, and Brandi was the maid of honor.

Sharla said it, maybe a little too loudly and too often in Fifi's hearing.

"This is how it was supposed to be. This is perfect!"

Fifi didn't mind. She was basking in her mother of the bride status. She was also contemplating her own wedding to Jules. As for Jules, he gave away the bride, a huge smile on his face.

"That's the last one of the boys to tie the knot," Pastor

Tate said to his wife, Adalynn. They were at the reception, "I am so happy for the boys. They deserve all the happiness, considering how they began."

Adalynn nodded. "Now for Monique's girls. I wonder how they will end up. I worry about them, you know. Will they find love like their cousins, will any of them settle down with families?"

"I know," Pastor Tate muttered. "They haven't exactly had an easy time of it, have they?"

"No," Adalynn muttered not at all, "but today is Case's day. A day to think positive thoughts and to celebrate his love for Lyla."

"I agree," Tate touched his glass to hers. "To Case and Lyla."

"To Case and Lyla. May they be blessed with many years of love and laughter." Adalynn touched her glass to his.

The End

Author's Notes

Dear Reader,

Thank you for reading A Case of Love. The individual stories for the Wiley Brothers are over. However, the Pryce Sisters are coming up and the Wiley Brothers will be featured in those stories, so you can still keep up with the family.

An excerpt of Giselle's story, Baby For A Pryce, is on the next page. This time I won't leave you waiting long.

As usual, thank you for reading my work. Don't forget to leave a review on Case of Love. Reviews are much appreciated.

Thanks again. All the best,

Brenda

Here is an excerpt from Baby For A Pryce (Pryce Sisters Book 1)

Just one more lap. Giselle thought as she ran around the track. One more step. One more push. She stopped. She couldn't make it. No amount of inspiration was going to make her get there. Her legs felt as if they didn't belong to her.

She was tired and drained, inexplicably so.

"Come on Gis," Kurt urged her on. He jogged past her and then turned around. "What's up with you today? Feeling sick?"

"I don't know." Giselle sat down in the middle of the track and stretched, "I cannot go another minute. I might be coming down with something."

Kurt frowned. "That's been happening a lot lately. Are you subconsciously choosing medicine over tracks?"

"Why would you say that?" Giselle frowned. "I train every day!"

"And you are progressively getting worse." Kurt snorted. "You knocked over five hurdles yesterday. Your time has dropped to what you used to run in high school, which was way past a minute. I have a hunch that this is more mental than physical."

"I don't know. Maybe. I am just not feeling it." Giselle panted. "I just want to go home, have something to eat and crash."

"Are you sure this has nothing to do with the brand-new shiny scholarships that you got today?" Kurt sneered, "are you sure that you are not listening to the sweet, serene call of med school and now you have mentally exited the will to do tracks?"

"How did you know about the scholarships?" Giselle glared at Kurt Yu, her coach and now tormentor. The scholarships were supposed to be a secret until she decided to reveal it.

Kurt stopped jogging on the spot and folded his arms. "Everybody is celebrating your accomplishment in the Science building. Giselle Pryce got not one but two scholarships. She is a genius and so pretty too. Oh, joy and delight!"

Giselle chuckled. "Look happier for my success, Coach."

"I look like this all the time. I do not have a smiley face. Deep down inside a generous part of me is rejoicing at your success. Deep, deep, down."

Kurt slumped beside her on the tracks and groaned. "You were doing so well. We could have gone pro. Now you are going to be a sports doctor. Where's the fun in that?"

"I didn't say I was going to take up the offers." Giselle watched as Kurt shook his head from side to side and pulled his fingers through his overlong curls.

He was half Nigerian, half Korean, and he was tall and muscular, not too heavy or too thin, he had the slanted eyes from his Asian father and thick curly hair from his African mother.

He mocked her, repeating what she said in a high-pitched exaggerated facsimile of her voice. "I didn't say I was going to take up the offers. You would be crazy not to. I wish..."

"You wish I wasn't so smart?" Giselle teased.

"Yeah." Kurt scowled.

In a way, she understood what he was saying. He had asked her a year ago if she was serious about tracks because he didn't want her to waste his time coaching her, but she had given him an emphatic, 'Yes.'

No athlete was more serious than she was about tracks and especially her pet event the four-hundred-meter hurdles.

Kurt had been skeptical, but he had become her coach, and they had gotten some good results. She had medaled in a few international events.

"I was almost sure I had another 400-meter hurdles champion on my hands. We were this close." He pinched his fingers together. "This close. We would go professional. I could bask in your limelight. Train some other high paying stars… make a couple of millions…we'd get married have a couple of high performing children. I would train them too and ride the gravy train into retirement."

Giselle laughed. "Kurt you say that to all the girls."

"No," Kurt said seriously, "just you. We shouldn't have broken up."

"But we did. Talking about it is like beating a dead dog." Giselle sighed and got up. "I am going home."

"Wait!" Kurt got up too. "You said that you weren't feeling well. Don't you want to check it out with the school doctor."

"No." Giselle shook her head. "I think my issue is lack of rest. I need some, and I need it badly. I am going to ask Pete to pick me up. He could give me a lift home. Tiana borrowed my car this morning."

Giselle pulled out her phone to text Pete. He was just across the street at the university. She knew he had evening classes.

Can I get a lift? T has my car. She texted.

"Peter Wiley," Kurt sneered, "I don't know what you see in that boy."

"He is not a boy," Giselle growled. "If you saw him recently, you wouldn't say that, and he is doing classes at the university now."

"A college freshman." Kurt snorted. "You left me for a college freshman."

"We didn't break up because of Pete," Giselle said crossly. "And I told you he is off topic. I don't care who you see since we broke up."

"That's because I haven't been in a relationship with anyone," Kurt growled. "I don't spend all my waking moments trying to rob the cradle."

Giselle giggled. "You are three years older than I am, were you robbing the cradle when we were dating?"

Kurt glared at her. "I think this Pete person is bad news. He is distracting. He is young, and he is a college freshman. You just graduated from college. You have ivy league scholarships. You won a bronze medal at the CARIFTA games. You are too good for him."

Giselle glanced at her phone when it pinged. In the parking lot.

She could see Pete's black SUV through the chain link fence that separated the training area, from the parking lot.

He was sitting with the window down. He was probably waiting for Giselle to finish training. It had slipped her mind that she had told him that Tiana was going to have her car all day.

Her eyes softened at the sight of him. He was thoughtful as usual. Pete was mature beyond his years and more in tuned to her needs than anyone else.

Kurt followed closely behind her. "Oh there is lover boy, and I do mean it literally. He is a boy, and he was spying on you. Probably insecure and jealous about us."

"Shut up, Kurt," Giselle growled. "Stop it, Pete is not up for discussion."

"You aren't sleeping with him, are you Gis?" Kurt asked suspiciously. "Is he the reason that you suddenly aren't focused on training?"

Giselle stopped walking and said as forcefully as she could. "That is none of your business!"

Kurt said just as fiercely. "You are my most promising

athlete. It worries me when you are not focused!"

"I will be fine." Giselle turned toward the gate. "My life will unfold the way it is supposed to unfold."

Kurt glanced across at the parking lot again. Pete had exited the vehicle and was walking toward them. Kurt understood what Giselle was talking about. He didn't look like a boy. He had come into his own. He was leanly muscular, tall, handsome and he knew it. He was walking like a man who knew his worth.

The girls playing netball on the other side of the parking lot had stopped training and were cat calling him. "Hey, handsome!"

"So repugnant," Kurt muttered. "Somebody needs to speak to those women about their harassment."

Giselle grinned. "Bye Kurt. Stop worrying. I promise I will be fine by tomorrow."

OTHER BOOKS BY BRENDA BARRETT

Pryce Sisters Series

Baby For A Pryce (Book 1)- Giselle Pryce had a bright future, two scholarships from Ivy League schools and a track career that was going somewhere, when she discovered she was pregnant. She had several decisions to make.

Right Pryce Wrong Time (Book 2)- Tiana got her high school teacher James fired for inappropriate conduct because of her jealousy. When she meets him again as an adult in a different situation, she has no idea how to act.

Yours, For A Pryce (Book 3)- Toddy Pryce offers his favorite sister Elsa to his young political rival Mason Magnus in exchange to not run against him in the next elections.

Wiley Brothers Series

Between Brothers (Book 0)- The beginning of the Wiley brothers saga, Joseph Wiley's unconventional family life may prove to be fatal to some members of the family.

For Pete's Sake (Book 1)- Preston has a run in with a child named Pete who claims that he is the grandson of their former housekeeper Pamela Stone.

Crossing Jordan (Book 2)- Jordan is miffed when Shawn takes her new fiancé to Jamaica and insists that he be man of honor at their wedding.

Fire and Walter (Book 3)- Walter's past came rushing to greet him shortly after his appointment as church elder. The new pastor was his childhood molestor, his wife was his ex from college and her cousin was the girl who got away. Walter had a lot of decisions to make.

The Perfect Guy (Book 4) - After a patient five years waiting for Lucia, Guy had his work cut out for him to prove himself worthy of her affections. He had played the part of poor farmer for too long and now he had competition in the form of the handsome doctor Ace Jackson.

The Patience of A Saint (Book 5)- Something was wrong with Saint's wife Sandrene. It didn't take a genius to see that she was changed beyond all recognition. Saint had to get to the bottom of it, before it was too late for them to salvage anything from the relationship.

A Case of Love (Book 6)- After a concert, Case is offered a girl to buy. Her fate was in his hands. He could keep her or leave her to the mercy of her evil family.

Resetter Series

Never Too Late (Book 1)- Addi finds out she is a resetter and goes back to the summer of 92 to change her family's lives.

Never Say Never (Book 2)- Skyler's handsome college lecturer, who happens to be her neighbor, has a 't' in his palms. Should she tell him the significance of it. If she does, would he believe her?

Now or Never (Book 3)- Ten years later Addi and Randy meet again at Randy's engagement party. Why is it that the chemistry between them was still so potent? Can they ever have a future together? Would Randy choose her this time around?

Almost Never (Book 4)- Tech genius Joshua Porter had all but given up on love. He then meets Portia, an inmate at the female penitentiary and his life takes a turn for the adventurous.

The Scarlett Family Series

Scarlett Baby (Book 1)- When the head of the Scarlett family died, Yuri had to return home to Treasure Beach for the funeral. What he didn't count on was seeing Marla, his childhood sweetheart and his best friend's wife. And when emotions overwhelm them and a few months later Marla is pregnant, Yuri wants the impossible: his best friend's wife and the baby they made together...

Scarlett Sinner (Book 2)- Pastor Troy Scarlett realizes the hard way that some sins are bound to be revealed, like the child that he had out of wedlock with his wife's mortal enemy from college. His wife Chelsea was not happy with the status quo. She was not taking care of the son of the woman she had so despised from college. And she could not get over the deep betrayal that she felt from her husband's indiscretion.

Scarlett Secret (Book 3)- Terri Scarlett had a soft spot for her friend, Lola. She was funny and sweet and they looked remarkably alike. But when Lola's Arab prince demands his bride, Terri foolishly exchange places with her friend and they meet up on a world of trouble.

Scarlett Love (Book 4)- Slater always looked forward to delivering packages to the law firm where he could get a glimpse of the stunning female lawyer, Amoy Gardener. Unfortunately, for Slater a woman like Amoy would not take him seriously, especially when she found out that he could not read!

Scarlett Promise (Book 5)- Driven by desperation Lisa Barclay decides to make some extra money by prostituting herself after being kicked out in the streets. Her first customer turns out to be a popular government senator and then to her horror he dies...

Scarlett Bride (Book 6)- When Oliver Scarlett's missionary work in the Congo region was coming to an end, he had a decision to make, marry Ashaki Azanga and save her from being the fourth wife to the chief of the village or leave her to her fate and get on with his life...

Scarlett Heart (Book 7)- After receiving a heart transplant shy librarian Noah Scarlett started to take on character traits that were unlike him and he kept dreaming of a girl named Cassandra Green...

Rebound Series

On The Rebound- For Better or Worse, Brandon vowed to stay with Ashley, but when worse got too much he moved out and met Nadine. For the first time in years he felt happy, but then Ashley remembered her wedding vows...

On The Rebound 2- Ashley reinvented herself and was now a first lady in a country church in Primrose Hill, but her obsessed ex friend Regina showed up and started digging into the lives of the saints at church. Somebody didn't like Regina's digging. Someone had secrets that were shocking enough to kill for...

Magnolia Sisters

Dear Mystery Guy (Book 1)- Della Gold details her life in a journal dedicated to a mystery guy. But when fascination turns into obsession she finds herself wanting to learn even more about him but in her pursuit of the mystery guy she begins to learn more about herself...

Bad Girl Blues (Book 2)- Brigid Manderson wanted to go to med school but for the time being she was an escort working for her mother, an ex-prostitute. When her latest customer offers her the opportunity of a lifetime would she take it? Or would she choose the harder path and uncertain love with a Christian guy?

Her Mistaken Dreams (Book 3)- Caitlin Denvers dream guy had serious issues. He has a dead wife in his past and he was the main suspect in her murder. Did he really do it? Or did Caitlin for the first time have a mistaken dream?

Just Like Yesterday (Book 4)- Hazel Brown lost six months of memory including the summer that she conceived her son, and had no idea who his father could be. Now that she had the means to fight to get him back from the Deckers, she finds out that the handsome Curtis Decker is willing to share her son with her after all.

passionate Bancroft, the creative loner who didn't mind living dangerously; but when a terrible thing happened to her at her friend Tracy's party, it changed her. She found that courting rumors can be devastating and that only the truth could set her free.

A Younger Man (Book 7)- Pastor Vanley Bancroft loved Anita Parkinson despite their fifteen-year age gap, but Anita had a secret, one that she could not reveal to Vanley. To tell him would change his feelings toward her, or force him to give up the ministry that he loved so much.

Just To See Her (Book 8)- Jessica Bancroft had the opportunity to meet her fantasy guy Khaled, he was finally coming to Mount Faith but she had feelings for Clay Reid, a guy who had all the qualities she was looking for. Who would she choose and what about the weird fascination Khaled had for Clay?

The Three Rivers Series

Private Sins (Book 1)- Kelly, the first lady at Three Rivers Church was pregnant for the first elder of her church. Could she keep the secret from her husband and pretend that all was well?

Loving Mr. Wright (Book 2)- Erica saw one last opportunity to ditch her single life when Caleb Wright appeared in her town. He was perfect for her, but what was he hiding?

Unholy Matrimony (Book 3) - Phoebe had a problem, she was poor and unhappy. Her solution to marry a rich man was derailed along the way with her feelings for Charles Black, the poor guy next door.

If It Ain't Broke (Book 4)- Chris Donahue wanted a place in his child's life. Pinky Black just wanted his love. She also wanted him to forget his obsession with Kelly and love her. That shouldn't be so hard? Should it?

Contemporary Romance/Drama

After The End--Torn between two lovers. Colleen married her high school sweetheart, Isaiah, hoping that they would live happily ever after but life intruded and Isaiah disappeared at sea. She found work with the rich and handsome, Enrique Lopez, as a housekeeper and realized that she couldn't keep him at arms length...

Love Triangle: Three Sides To The Story- George, the husband, Marie, the wife and Karen-the mistress. They all get to tell their side of the story.

The Preacher And The Prostitute - Prostitution and the clergy don't mix. Tell that to ex-prostitute, Maribel, who finds herself in love with the Pastor at her church. Can an ex-prostitute and a pastor have a future together?

New Beginnings - Inner city girl Geneva was offered an opportunity of a lifetime when she found out that her 'real' father was a very wealthy man. Her decision to live up-town meant that she had to leave Froggie, her 'ghetto don,' behind. She also found herself battling with her stepmother and battling her emotions for Justin, a suave up-towner.

Full Circle- After graduating from university, Diana

wanted to return to Jamaica to find her siblings. What she didn't foresee was that she would meet Robert Cassidy and that both their pasts would be intertwined, and that disturbing questions would pop up about their parentage, just when they were getting close.

Historical Fiction/Romance

The Empty Hammock- Workaholic, Ana Mendez, fell asleep in a hammock and woke up in the year 1494. It was the time of the Tainos, a time when life seemed simpler, but Ana knew that all of that was about to change.

The Pull Of Freedom- Even in bondage the people, freshly arrived from Africa, considered themselves free. Led by Nanny and Cudjoe the slaves escaped the Simmonds' plantation and went in different directions to forge their destiny in the new country called Jamaica.

Jamaican Comedy (Material contains Jamaican dialect)

Di Taxi Ride And Other Stories- Di Taxi Ride and Other Stories is a collection of twelve witty and fast paced short stories. Each story tells of a unique slice of Jamaican life.